Mabel Leigh Hunt

CUPOLA HOUSE

Illustrated by Nora S. Unwin

J. B. Lippincott Company

PHILADELPHIA AND NEW YORK

jH 916cw

Contents

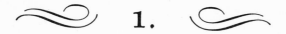

1.

The Arrival

"HO, HUM!" sighed Lizette from the back seat of the family surrey. And she added a groan, for out of her grumpiness she wanted everyone to know how tired she was of the grind of wheels and the clop of hoofs. She was tired of the heat and sun-dazzle. Every nine-year-old inch of her was thoroughly bored with *not getting there*. The jollity she had shared with Max and Martin in the early stages of the journey, when they sang rounds, played word-games, and giggled over tongue-twisters, had sunk into weariness.

From the front seat beside Papa the twins also breathed out matching sighs. "It feels like a year since we left our old home in Fairland this morning," grumbled Max.

"Yes, a whole year!" yawned Martin. "I bet it's 1907 right now, instead of 1906." The boys punched one another in sudden delight at their own remarks, which they considered funny.

"We could've got there a lot quicker if we had an automobile," declared Max. "I bet I could go as fast on my own two feet as old Silas has gone on four."

"But you couldn't pull a carriage-load of people as Silas has done steadily, mile after mile," Papa said. "An automobile is too new and

9

imperfect an invention to be trusted by a busy doctor. Just imagine me answering a call any rainy night, and my automobile bogging down in the mud, or being flooded as I try to ford a creek. No, I'll trust my light road cart and Molly, my fast little mare."

Lizette lifted herself lazily and peered past Papa, the twins, and Silas's ears to look at Uncle Greg, driving Molly from Papa's one-seater cart. Beside him sat Evvie. Beneath her straw sailor Evvie's thick red braids tossed to and fro. She was eleven and a half, and as always, appeared her sensible, independent self. The sight of her, so perky and unwearied, seemed to add to Lizette's discouragement. "Ho, hum," she sighed again.

Mamma, seated beside her, leaned a little closer to give her a comforting hug. She reached forward and patted the shoulders of the twins. "There's no use grumbling about the length of the journey," she said, "though I'm a bit tired myself, and so, no doubt, is Papa." Mamma spanked a tiny yawn back into her mouth. But suddenly she brightened. "If I'm not mistaken," she said, "I think I see the college towers peeping above the treetops away over yonder."

"That's right, you do," answered Papa. "And if the mopey youngsters in this carriage are ever to cheer up, now is the time, for we are arriving!" Papa pointed toward a large roadside sign.

WELCOME TO WINFIELD
HOME OF ADAIR UNIVERSITY

At last! Even in the torrid July heat, Lizette felt chills of excitement. She caught up her leghorn hat, donned it, and snapped the rubber under her chin. In a moment this unknown town of Winfield would witness the arrival of Doctor John Hudson and his household. In a dither of family pride, Lizette wished they were not all so dusty. The faces of the twins were actually grimy.

Ahead, she saw Evvie turn and wave excitedly as country suddenly became town. "Jiminy, *pavement!*" cried Max, his eyes popping. It was true. What a wonder that Silas, his hoofs ringing smartly on the hard surface, didn't swivel around and whinny, "Look, Family— *asphalt*—something we never had in Fairland!"

"Yonder is the university," said Papa. The campus was quiet, deep in grass, with broad-armed trees casting long shadows. Gracious old buildings, closed for the summer, were half-smothered in ivy. Suddenly from the clock tower the bell struck five deep mellow notes. How pure and serene a sound—like five noble words of welcome falling into the hearts of the newcomers! Speechless, Papa turned and looked at Mamma. "Lovely!" she murmured. "Living in a university town!" Then Mamma, who had wept on leaving Fairland this morning, *did* want to come to Winfield, after all! Lizette felt stabbed with a quick little arrow of joy.

Papa flicked the whip and began driving fast. "Keep your eyes open, everyone," he called. "We're now on Bishop Street, and at the very end of it stands our new home."

Now—the very end! With a fresh burst of speed, the horse swung his fat glistening rump, dashed across Auburn Road, and into a long driveway paved with cinders. The family had a hurried view of green, woodsy space. Through plumy, interlacing boughs they caught glimpses of the house. Something glittered on top. In a perfectly exhilarating climax the surrey swept around a turn and halted at a tall elm tree. Out spilled the passengers to join Unc and Evvie. Gaily they trooped to the front lawn. "Whew! What a big house!" they gasped.

"*Only* eighteen rooms," chuckled Papa. "The house is so big it deserves a name all its own."

Uncle Greg spoke up. "Big inside and out, what with those eight verandahs adding to its spread. And kids, think what fun you will have in that whale of a barn! You haven't seen the elegant chicken house, and there's a woodshed for spankings." Unc gave the twins a wicked wink as he waved his hand around. "Fifteen acres of fields, gardens and orchards for you to roam over, and a pasture with an honest-to-goodness pond." Followed by the wide-eyed gaze of the children, Unc swaggered up and unlocked the front door.

But Mamma stood still. "Mercy!" she cried, her hand at her throat. "I knew it was a big house, but—think of the fuel, think of the housekeeping! However in the world shall we—" Suddenly speechless, Mamma gazed up at the square white house standing proudly on its double terrace. In the light from the westering sun, the great twin chimneys glowed rosy-red. The windows of the cupola crowning the roof glittered with fiery light.

"Edith, just look around you," said Papa, anxiously imploring Mamma's approval. "Did you ever see such magnificent trees—the noble spruces, the fine maples?"

Mamma's slow gaze turned to Papa, then to the youngsters clustered around. Again her glance swept over the big waiting house. She gave a little sigh, then slipping her hand within Papa's, she said quietly, "Come what will, but with God's help, this is a house where we shall be happy."

It sounded like church, like the benediction at the end, when one feels blessed and in good keeping.

Suddenly the twins had but a single thought. "There must be a way to get up there!" they shouted. "We've gotta see the little house on the roof!"

"I'm coming, too," cried Evvie, snatching off her hat.

"Wait for me!" Lizette plunged forward, her leghorn hanging on her shoulders.

Oh, it was thrilling to run through halls and stairways they had never seen before, with glimpses of furniture standing in unfamiliar places like ghosts. On the second floor the boys jerked open several doors before they found the right one. They knew it because of the shaft of light falling down through a narrow, enclosed staircase. Up they scampered with their sisters, across the shallow, dark-cornered attic, then mounted a short, ladder-like flight. And there they were! To their delight, Uncle Greg was close on their heels, to witness their joyful astonishment at the cupola. That is what he said it was called.

The cupola was a peaked, four-sided dome supplied with fourteen narrow windows. It seemed to be fashioned entirely of glass and was now flooded with golden light. The children leaped to the narrow seat which ran around under the windows, to kneel there and press their noses against the sun-heated panes. "Look!" they shouted, "oh, look!" The lofty view over the tops of the trees seemed breathlessly exciting. The children tried opening the windows, but they were nailed tight.

"Nobody ever had a house with a cupola! Nobody but us!" cried Lizette.

"You're mistaken," said Unc. "There are others here and there, built around the same time as this—forty or fifty years ago. But none more handsome than this one, I feel certain."

"There may be cupolas, but how many kids have a real-for-sure pond right on their own grounds?" asked Max. "C'm on, Marty, let's go and look at it." The feet of the twins were suddenly noisy on the stairs.

But Evvie and Lizette lingered with Unc. The excitement of completely exploring house and grounds lay ahead, but surely nothing could be more thrilling than the cupola. "Papa said the house should have a name of its own," mused Lizette. "We could call it *Cupo—*"

"We could call it *Cupola House!*" cried Evvie. She hadn't borrowed the idea from Lizette. It had simply popped into her head the same instant.

"It's the very name, the *only* name!" Unc's face was bright with approval.

"Mamma! Papa!" screamed Lizette, pecking on a window-pane.

"We've named the house!" shrieked Evvie, her knuckles also tapping. Papa and Mamma, still on the terrace, were so far below that their figures looked squat. They glanced up in answer to the frantic summons. But they couldn't make out what the girls were saying.

"Well anyway, they can't help but love the name when they do hear it," gloated Evvie. "Oh, I just feel glorious at the very tiptop of Cupola House!"

"Me, too," agreed Lizette, spinning on one heel. "I just feel heavenly! I feel like the princess Rapunzel in her fairy tower!"

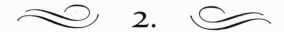

2.

View from the Cupola

SO THE Hudsons called it Cupola House. Papa said the name should be pronounced correctly. "Look it up," he advised.

The big dictionary on its stand was part of the library furniture. The children regarded it with a little dislike, because Mamma and Papa expected them to be more chummy with it than they had time for. But they respected it, for it knew everything, yet was so magnificently silent about it. No boastful chatter from that dictionary! But what a Niagara of words it could spill out were it given speech. Lizette had sometimes thought about it. Now, obedient to Papa, she and her brothers gathered around to watch Evvie's forefinger move down the column of words beginning with *c*. They listened as she experimented with syllables. "It's pronounced *koo-puh-lah*," she announced, "and it means *a small dome, or, any small structure on the top of a building for ornamental or other purpose*. I wonder," Evvie went on, "is our cupola 'ornamental, or for other purposes'?"

"It's meant to be exciting and to have fun in," declared Lizette, certain she was speaking for everyone.

"It would be more fun if we could open the windows and get some air in the cupola," Max complained.

"And maybe climb out on the roof," Martin suggested.

"Twins!" warned Mamma. "The roof is very high above the ground. Don't ever let me hear of you on that roof."

"Don't worry," Papa assured her. "Even a pair of ten-year-olds couldn't get those windows unfastened. As to Evvie's question, the cupola is part of the architectural plan of the house. In other words, the house wouldn't be itself, nor look complete without it, although it is useless as far as serving a purpose."

So the cupola was like the star on a Christmas tree, or, to Lizette, like a fairy tower. It was the ornament crowning a house which was thrilling to the children in its newness and size. The house and cupola, the big barn and ample grounds—all had surely been planned as a wonderful play place for children.

But alas, during ten days of hard work it took every pair of young hands to help Mamma get the house in order. Once or twice Lizette vanished completely to avoid some chore she didn't care for. But Evvie treated her with such scorn she didn't try the ruse again. Not that Evvie wanted to work every minute, either. During a brief game of wood-tag one day, she said, "We wouldn't have time to play at all if it weren't for my Unc."

"*Your* Unc!" cried Lizette. "Just because you both have red hair, you think he's all yours. He's our Unc, too!"

The special warmth between Evvie and Unc was such an everyday matter that Lizette's little flare-up of jealousy was scarcely noticed, as everyone agreed on what a help Unc had been in the moving. Mamma declared she didn't know what she would have done without him. Unc poked a good deal of fun at himself because he was supposed to be on vacation from his work in Torbridge, the big town forty miles east of Winfield. "Vacation my foot!" he joked. "I've never worked harder in my life."

Papa was of little help. He was getting his medical books and equipment unpacked and arranged in his office. It was a mile away, and overlooked Winfield's courthouse square from the second floor of a business building. So it was Unc and Mamma who washed miles of woodwork and tacked down yards of carpet. In the evenings Unc and Papa took turns mowing grass. The children ran endless errands. They scrubbed verandahs and brick walks. Mamma and the girls polished furniture and washed china. Unc cleaned the many windows. The children polished the reachable ones with wads of crumpled paper.

At last Mamma pronounced everything finished. She looked dreadfully tired. She had even lost weight. "I can't go another step until I've rested in bed for at least half a day," she announced. "I mean this very afternoon. I just wonder," she added, thoughtfully, "if this house may not be too much for one woman."

The children looked so shocked at having the least fault found with the house that she added, "How I love the smell of soap and polish! And doesn't everything look shining and beautiful?"

Unc pretended to curl his lip, although he, too, felt pride in the appearance of the handsome big rooms. "Kids, do you realize we haven't yet cleaned the cupola?" he asked.

"Let us help!" The children showed such unwonted eagerness that Unc laughed. They sang *Meet Me In St. Louis* all the way to the top of the house. But the brooms and brushes raised so much dust within the cupola that the singing changed to sneezing. When the dust settled, it was time to wash the windows.

Unc pried one open so that he could step to the roof and clean outside. "You're not even to lean out, hear me?" he cautioned the children. "See how steeply the roof slopes to the eaves. Lose your balance and you'd go rolling until—*plunk!*—you'd roll off the edge and strike the sidewalk below. Then we'd have a funeral!"

The children whooped. It was somehow hilarious to imagine such a thing as a Hudson child rolling off the roof and becoming a corpse. And now, with the window opened and the fresh air streaming in, the children felt giddy with excitement. They sky-larked around in the lofty space, bumping into one another, making faces at Unc through the windows, and shrieking at the horrible grimaces he made in return.

The fun went to Martin's head. While Unc scrubbed and polished on the far side of the cupola, the boy flung one leg over the sill of the open window. He hopped lightly to the roof. His foot slipped in a pool of suds left on the slates by Unc. Down went Martin, sliding rapidly to the place where the gutters edged fatal space.

For an instant the other children were struck dumb. Then they began screaming, "Unc! Unc!"

Their uncle had already seen Martin disappear below the level of the cupola. He shouted, started to the rescue, and overturned his pail of water. Trying to catch it, he lost his footing. Then didn't Unc himself slip on the slates opposite to Martin's toboggan slide? It was unbelievable! The children were afraid to look. Yet their heads whirled to the north roof, where Unc was scooting, then to the south, the direction of Martin's tumble. But there! By great good luck Martin had lodged against the base of a chimney. "Don't move, Marty, don't move! Unc will save you!" screamed Evvie.

What faith! It was because Unc was Unc. Nothing final could happen to him. And indeed when the children looked again they saw that Unc had managed to halt his slide. They saw him sit up, cautiously, and jerk off his shoes and socks. He gave them a toss. They flew over the edge of the roof, as the water pail had done under its own power. Now Unc rose up, turned around with wary balance, and mounted the slope in his bare feet. Reaching the cupola,

he braced himself for a shock. Then he saw Martin, frightened, but alive and whole. Unc's face, so pale that the freckles stood out like sprinkles of cinnamon, suddenly turned brick red. His very hair seemed to flame brighter. "Hold on, you little cuss!" yelled Unc. *Oh, jiminy, Unc's temper is up! Looky, Unc is blazing mad at Martin!*

Like an angry bear backing down a tree trunk, Unc backed on all fours to Martin's chimney, and pulled him to his feet. Gripping the boy's arm, Unc hauled him up the roof with surprising speed, for the slates were burning hot. He boosted Martin through the cupola's open window and climbed in after him. Unc lowered himself to the seat. Unc turned Martin over his knee. *Whack, whack* went the back of a scrubbing brush on Martin's sitting-down place. *Eek, eek,* squeaked Martin at every whack. But he wouldn't shed a tear.

Max looked the other way, gritting his teeth in sympathy for his twin. Evvie also turned her back. Spanking is a private matter. Staring isn't done. But when inflicted by someone as crackajack as Unc on someone as disobedient as Martin, spanking is a just thing to be endured by relatives as sensibly as possible. Evvie, who was almost always sensible, knew this quite well.

But Lizette, who ran away from trouble when she could, scuttled down three flights of stairs, peeped into Mamma's room, and found her still sleeping. Lizette felt suddenly bereft. What should she do with herself? The home library was a pleasant place. She could sit in the red velvet chair and read a fairy tale out of the Brothers Grimm. But Martin's sin, Unc's anger, and Mamma forsaking everyone and everything for sleep, made Lizette long for a different sort of comfort than could be found in a book.

3.

A Welcome for Lizette

GRAVELY she washed her hands and face at the kitchen tap. She walked through the house and seated herself on the steps of the south verandah. At the end of the walk and across the Hudson driveway stood a white picket fence. Lizette had been telling herself that she would some day open its gate and trip through, alone. But it took courage for a shy girl. Max and Martin had breezed through the gate twice a day to bring back the milk the Hudsons needed until Papa could buy a cow. Evvie, in friendly curiosity, had once visited the other side of the gate and returned with a bouquet of spicy old-fashioned pinks. Mamma had been invited to come and carry home gifts of flaky biscuit, waxy gingerbread, and once, a custard float that melted on the tongue like delicious foam. Lizette had heard Mamma rejoice because of the good neighbors beyond that gate.

Now Lizette sat gazing at a scene which might have come out of a never-never land—a snug, vine-wreathed cottage set amidst flowers and green bowers. It was the sort of cottage that lost wandering maidens come upon, by lucky chance, in the depths of forests. And Mr. and Mrs. Van Winkle, whom Lizette had seen from a distance, bore a remarkable resemblance to the eternal woodsman and his wife, quiet and simple and kind. Perhaps if Lizette pretended to be a little slavey who had to run away from home because her step-mother lay abed all the time, she could really enter that gate. The kind woodsman's wife would welcome, feed, and pamper her.

Lizette got up a little uncertainly. She began hopping down the south walk on one foot to defy the 'fraidy-cat inside of her. Crossing the cindery lane, she laid her hand on the Van Winkle gate. If it had suddenly sprung into leaf and bud under her touch, she would not have been surprised, so full of sudden magic did the moment seem. Softly she raised the latch, pushed open the gate, and slipped through. There were stepping stones half-buried in the grass. Lizette hopped from one to the next, pretending that swift, dark forest waters flowed under her feet. On the last stone she paused, timidly, and there came to her a fragrance of fresh baking mingled with the scent of garden flowers.

Suddenly Lizette was no longer afraid, so welcoming did the wood-cutter's cottage seem. She knocked on the kitchen door. The clean, bare boards of the back entry creaked under a heavy tread, and Mrs. Van Winkle, rosy and plump in a blue-checkered apron, hove into view. Without saying a word, but beaming with kindness, she reached out and pushed open the screen. In the kitchen, still in a sunny kind of silence, she handed Lizette a saucer-sized cooky. It had been baked with a sprinkling of red sugar, which gave it a complexion very like Mrs. Van Winkle's.

"Shall we have a little set-down?" she suggested in a low, soft voice. She led the way into the sitting-room and lowered her plumpness into a chair by the window. Lizette sat opposite in a small, folding rocker, basking in the warmth of her hostess' smile. There were no tiresome questions, such as what-is-your-name, how-old-are-you, are-you-a-good-girl?

Lizette's brown eyes roved, and she saw that the inside of the cottage was altogether right, too. The rag carpet was gay. Painted on the door of the mantel clock was a lilac-colored dove, with wings spread and a green twig in its beak. Across a sofa lay a crazy-quilt that was like a hundred rainbows broken up in tiny patches and sewed together again with golden flashes of feather-stitching. The room was full of summer light and the smell of fresh baking.

"Is Mr. Van Winkle a woodcutter?" asked Lizette, at last.

"He cuts wood sometimes," answered Mrs. Van. "He can turn his hand to 'most any chore. But I reckon he's more of a small farmer than anything."

At least he's part woodcutter, thought Lizette. She rocked, feeling completely at home. Over her flowed the certainty that she had opened the gate to a place of perfect peace and kindness—a very special place for Lizette Hudson.

"I'm Lizette," she said, "and I live across the lane at Cupola House. In Fairland, my papa was a very busy doctor. But he gave up all that and moved us to Winfield because of better schools here. When we're old enough, we'll even go to the university up the street. My Uncle Greg was dead set against our moving. He said there were already plenty of doctors in Winfield," babbled Lizette, rashly spilling out private family talk. "So maybe we shall be poor," she added. And for a moment, with a small shiver of relish, she imagined herself as someone like the little match girl, who not only starved to death, but froze. "Do you have any books for girls my age?" she went on. Her glance fell on a long narrow volume lying on Mrs. Van's chair-side table.

"That's my day book," explained Mrs. Van. "I write in it about my flowers, people, and what I do and hear. That's my fountain pen in the little box." She said "fountain pen" as she might have said "that's my box of diamonds, emeralds and rubies."

"But I do have a few books," she went on. From one of the
cupboards that flanked the fireplace she drew a chunky volume
called *The Chatterbox*. "How nice and old-fashioned!" exclaimed
Lizette. She looked up at her hostess, and what she saw there, so
child-like and simple, caused her to offer the thing that to her meant
the closest of companionships. "I'll read to you if you like," she said.

Mrs. Van Winkle folded her hands across her stomach. Rocking
gently to and fro, she waited, as pleased as could be, for Lizette to
begin.

For a moment Lizette listened to the slow creak of the rocker,
to the quiet tick of the clock with its dove of peace. *The favorite
haunts of wild elephants*, began Lizette, *are in the depths of forest,
where they browse on bracken—*

Reading of elephants, Lizette heard a soft shuffling in the kitchen. "That you, P.D.?" called Mrs. Van, mildly.

P.D., who turned out to be Mr. Van Winkle, appeared in the doorway. He was in his shirt sleeves and wore a wide straw hat. "It's Lizette Hudson from next door," Mrs. Van explained, "so you needn't feel bashful. Change your hat, m' dear, an' come in an' rest your bones." Her tone was so tender it was a wonder the dove on the clock did not fly down to light on her finger. P.D. disappeared briefly and came back under a broad-brimmed hat of black felt. He seated himself in an armchair. As he fell into a doze, hat and all, Lizette noticed he had pink-sugar cheeks like those of his wife.

Lizette's eyes questioned her hostess as to whether further reading would disturb the woodcutter's rest. Mrs. Van assured her. "In his dreams P.D. will hear you and think you're a song sparrow."

Lizette accepted this as complimentary. Leafing through *The Chatterbox* she suddenly thought of something real that had storybook flavor. It had been puzzling her. "Did you know," she inquired, "that a knight lies buried in one corner of our north yard?"

Mrs. Van rocked. Lizette could tell she had never read a word about knights. "Somebody shining and brave and splendid," explained Lizette. "His name is *Sir Dragor, noblest of his kind, July, 1898*. That's what is printed, plain as day, on his headstone."

"I remember when Sir Dragor was buried," said Mrs. Van, calmly. Lizette was about to fall out of her chair with astonishment when Evvie suddenly appeared on the little front porch and peered through the screen door.

"Good afternoon, Mrs. Van Winkle," said Evvie, politely. "I am here to tell Lizette she is to come home. Lizette, Mamma has waked up. She is still tired and sleepy. So we're to have a picnic under the trees, out of left-overs and things. You and I are to help make sandwiches. Unc dressed and went uptown. The boys are off somewhere, but everybody will be home for the picnic supper. Won't it be fun?"

Lizette jumped to her feet so quickly she left the chair rocking behind her. A picnic! The Sir Dragor mystery could wait until another time.

4.

Family Matters

BESIDES sandwiches and left-overs there were tomatoes from the family vines for the picnic supper that evening. There was a watermelon from the family patch so crisp it crackled when Unc carved it. Max and Martin had brought a new boy home with them from their neighborhood explorations. His name was George Akers. He was nine years old. Martin informed the family that George was going to ride in the boat when he and Max got one for sailing on the pond. Everyone looked expectantly at Papa. "The pond is almost too small and shallow for a regular boat," he said. "Any kind of boat is expensive to buy just now. Maybe in a couple of years when my practice is flourishing you may have one."

"Great Scott, Papa, *two years!*" squealed Max. "That's ages! What say we build one ourselves, then?"

It didn't matter that no one answered, for at once the building of a boat became a firmly fixed ambition in the minds of the twins, and a hope in the minds of all others under twelve.

"I am glad we are having a picnic this evening instead of a funeral," declared Lizette.

Mamma's eyes opened in astonishment, and Papa asked what Lizette meant by such a shocking statement. Lizette had intended to explain about Martin and Unc on the roof. But glancing around, she saw secrecy veiling the faces of the twins and Evvie. Their eyes stared at her as cold as the eyes of fish. "I guess I was just talking to hear my head roar," she said, in a small voice.

"Max and I have been around since we cleaned the cupola," announced Martin, changing the subject adroitly. "The president of Adair University lives on the next corner. In the block after that there's a great Dane dog on a front porch. He looks like a statue. But he's alive. He's the biggest dog Max and I ever saw."

"That great Dane could bite a guy in two without half-trying," declared Max.

"He is kind of fierce-looking," agreed George. "But I never heard of him biting anybody."

"Anyway," Max went on, "in the same block as the dog there's a blind girl."

"Blind!" breathed Evvie, motherliness welling up within her. "I could lead her where she wants to go, and take care of her."

"Out places, yes," said George. "But inside her house you'd never guess she is blind. She knows just where everything is. She doesn't even have to hold out her hands to keep from bumping into things. Her name is Madge Ross. Her father teaches in the university."

"Well, tomorrow and after that, Marty and I are going to do lots more exploring," promised Max. "Then we'll be able to tell you anything you want to know about everybody and everything in Winfield."

"Watch your noses," warned Unc. "They'll grow a foot long from poking into other folks' business."

"Anyway, I have plans for tomorrow, "interrupted Mamma. "You have all worked hard helping to get the house in order. But we haven't had time for the vegetable garden. It is running to weeds. We must grub them out."

"Bright and early tomorrow," vowed Unc, "the kids and I will begin to grub."

"Max and George and I were gonna look for treasure in the pond," explained Martin. "No telling what's there. Somebody's gold ring, maybe, or a silver dollar lying on the bottom."

"There's more real treasure in a garden if it's made to yield," Papa pointed out.

"I'll help in the garden tomorrow," offered George.

"Great Scott!" cried the twins. In merry gratitude they flipped watermelon seeds at George.

"Now let me tell you young Hudsons the surprise we have for your mother." Papa's words drew quick attention.

"Your Uncle Greg and I had a talk in my office this afternoon. We decided that keeping this large house is too much for one woman, even with the good help of her children. Greg reminded me of someone who lives in the country not far from Fairland. So I called her by long distance. She has agreed to come to help cook and keep house. Her name is Addy Newton."

"How soon will she come? Shall we like her?"

"You mean—will she like *you?*" chuckled Unc.

"Can we afford to pay Addy's wages?" Mamma looked more worried than pleased. She knew the Winfield people had not yet begun to seek Papa's medical services.

"We'll manage." Papa tried to smile away Mamma's fears.

"Goody, we shan't have to work any more!" crowed Lizette.

"A princess you would ever be, reading old tales in the library," said Papa. "You'd be happier and more useful doing your share of the everyday work. I want you children to have time for play in this fine old place. But it won't be fine for long unless we all work to keep it that way. And Mamma," he added, "we must keep her, too. She is our most precious possession."

Mamma blushed. Unc clapped. The twins grinned. Evvie and Lizette ran to hug their mother.

"Suppose Evvie and I go in the surrey and bring Addy and her belongings," suggested Unc. "It will need to be soon, though, because I'm due in Torbridge any minute."

"There'd be room in the surrey for *other people*." Lizette couldn't help herself. Unc and Evvie, always pairing off!

"Thanks to everyone," said Papa, "but it's Doctor and Mrs. John Hudson who are going after Addy tomorrow. We shall enjoy seeing old friends in Fairland. On the way back we shall pick up Addy. You children will stay here. You may do whatever your uncle allows."

"I'll keep every one of them chained to their bedposts without food or water," growled Unc. His threat raised laughter.

"Mamma, be sure and tell the Fairland people about our cupola," urged Lizette, presently. "George, have you ever been up there? I will take you."

"I've seen that cupa*low* all my life," answered George, mispronouncing badly. "But I've never ackshally been in it."

"Run along, then," advised Mamma. "If I'm to go to Fairland tomorrow, I should cook some things tonight, so that Greg and my children may not starve while I am away."

The children were proud to escort George to the top of the house. It was the magic moment for it. The daylight, which at earth-level had already vanished, seemed to have gathered within the high glass cupola, to be held there, as pearly as light within a bubble.

Lizette tattled to George how Martin had stepped out of a cupola window, and what Unc had done about it. "You're always telling everything you know," muttered Martin, darkly. But George grinned at him with such understanding and admiration that the tattling did no harm to a friendship which was growing more satisfactory every minute. "Even if you did have a whacking," reasoned George, "it must've been exciting to roll down the roof, 'specially when you didn't go *smash* the whole way." And when he had gone downstairs with the others, George ran outside and looked up at the eaves, to measure with his wondering eye just how far Martin would have hurtled down if it hadn't been for the saving chimney.

By this time the twins were so enthusiastic about George that nothing would do but they persuade Papa to tell him "the story of Tig." The story, the cupola and the pond, which George had visited before supper, were the outstanding treats they could offer him. Seated on the shadowy north porch, while the fireflies winked among the branches of the pines, Papa began this favorite narrative of the Hudson children. They chimed in with anything he left out, for they knew the tale by heart. It had made a deep impression on Papa when as a boy he had heard it from his grandfather in North Carolina. Grandfather had actually known Tig, a Negro slave who had escaped when he learned he was to be sold. Tig's adventures were exciting, sad and funny. He had a gift of making his voice seem to come from the mouths of other people, or from other places, near or far. It helped him in his flight from those who tried to catch him. The hunger, dangers and hurts he suffered, and the freedom he finally enjoyed always aroused chills and thrills in the Hudson youngsters. Papa had imagination and a nice choice of words. He had great sympathy for Tig, and he knew the North Carolina country well.

This evening, after Papa finished, the spell of the story held everyone quiet for a little while. Then George let out such a deep sigh of enjoyment as to make the twins feel that George Akers, in the space of one evening, had become quite like a member of the Hudson family.

The girls also felt that George had become a brother. "Would you write in my autograph album?" asked Evvie. "Except when I can't help myself, I only ask people I really like." When George agreed, she told him how to spell *Evalina*. "It's my real name, and I like it," she confided. "But no one calls me anything but *Evvie,* and I simply hate it. When I get married, or maybe before, I'm going to change it to a name that can't be shortened."

George was reminded of a verse he had seen in a cousin's album. He scrawled, "When you get married and live on a farm, write me a letter as long as your arm."

The children were pleased with George's offering. It seemed to polish off the future so neatly.

5.

Of a Lonely Night

THE next morning seemed strange to the children, knowing, as their parents drove away in the surrey, that they would be orphans for two days and a night. But Unc was full of jokes during the weeding of the garden; he produced a bag of jelly beans for them to munch while slaving; just before noon he gave them a thorough cooling off with spray from the garden hose.

At noon Mrs. Van Winkle telephoned to offer a pan of hot corn-bread and a jar of fresh jelly. Lizette ran after them with all speed, because she also wanted to tell her friend the wonderful news that after tomorrow she would probably never have to wash or wipe another dish. Addy Newton, the new hired girl, would do them.

In the afternoon Martin and Max became joke-happy. They found a can of paint in the barn and colored all the green tomatoes on one of the vines a bright red. It was fun to be a little more wicked than usual and plague Unc as much as they dared.

After supper the boys ran off to the pond. Unc sprinkled the lawns. The girls cleared up the kitchen, which seemed drab and empty without Mamma. They played paper dolls on the south verandah steps. "This once," agreed Evvie, who believed herself too old for such play. But she knew Lizette was longing, the same as herself, for Mamma and Papa. In the evening shadows the big house loomed up strange and mysterious behind them. They were filled with a sense of the long, lonely night ahead.

As they sat hunched and quiet, a young man and a dog came across the lawn and up to the steps. Unc turned off the water and came around.

"I'm Thad Conroy," explained the young man. "I live up the street a short distance. I'm a junior in the university when school keeps." He laughed. "This is Anna, my great Dane. Tonight she has come to pay her respects to her noble dead ancestor. You may have noticed his grave on your place—Sir Dragor."

Unc patted the dog. Evvie, wonderfully emboldened, touched its proud flank, her fingers stiff and careful. Lizette shrank. Sir Dragor and Anna the great Dane—what could Thad Conroy mean?

Smiling, Unc led the way to the grave. The girls nipped along, a safe distance from Anna. As Lizette grew more and more confused about knights and great Danes, the twins came storming up. Even they did not greet Anna the same as other dogs. They stood off, respectfully admiring her size. Their feet and legs were streaked with mud from the pond. Martin reached into his pocket and tenderly drew forth a small checkered snake.

"Garter," he announced, proudly.

"Take that creature away somewhere," ordered Unc, "and go scrub yourselves." He gave each of the boys a determined push.

Off they went, with cheerful grins. After thinking about them for a heavy moment, Anna gave a single hoarse bark.

"Why did you bury Anna's father here?" asked Evvie.

"A tomboyish girl named Shirley Warren lived at this place before you came," answered Thad. "We used to play together. Shirley was crazy about Sir Dragor. We were about thirteen when he died, and nothing would do Shirley but to have him laid away at this spot. We had an elaborate funeral service, with all our goggle-eyed friends standing around. At the grave we sang *On the Banks of the Wabash*. It was mournful, and Shirley cried buckets." Thad laughed. "She persuaded her father to have this nifty headstone made and erected for Sir Dragor."

Unc laid his hand on Anna's head. "I'm sure I speak for the Hudsons, Anna, in inviting you to visit the resting-place of your noble father whenever you wish," he said, solemnly.

Lying between cool sheets in the bedroom a half hour later, Lizette could hear a murmur of talk going on between Unc and Thad. She thought of Anna as she had last seen her, posed like majestic bronze on the upper terrace. And she thought of the grave of Sir Dragor, lonely in its dark corner. It couldn't be a dog lying there—it couldn't be! It was a knight, rigid and splendid in his coat of mail. There was a giant sleeping in the north yard, too, under the myrtle plot. Papa himself had remarked that the thick mat of creeping plants was big enough for a giant's bed. Yes, at night the yard was a ghostly place with its shadowy spruces, its dead knight and sleeping giant. There had been nothing like it in Fairland, and Lizette wished that Mamma and Papa were at home. Beneath the sheet her hand crept along to find and grasp Evvie's braid. It was comforting. "Evvie," she whispered, "we left the paper dolls on the steps. Something might happen to them."

Evvie mumbled and turned over. After a moment she got up, staggering with sleep until she could get her balance. Lizette saw her gliding like a pale moth to the upper porch. She leaned over the railing. "Unc," she called, drowsily, "Lizette's paper dolls are on the step."

"I'll attend to them," promised Unc. Evvie came pattering back. Suddenly she gave a gasp, followed by a piercing shriek. Her flying leap into bed almost flattened Lizette. "Oh, mercy!" screamed Evvie. "I stepped on something awful!"

In a trice Unc and Thad Conroy were dashing up the stairs and into the room, with Anna leaping behind, as big as a calf. Unc switched on the ceiling light.

"Something cold and squirmy!" quavered Evvie. "I stepped on it!" She sat up, shuddering. Lizette also rose up, wide-eyed and a little green around the mouth. "It was a dragon," she whispered.

Unc and Thad began making a search. But it was the great Dane who first discovered where the dragon lay coiled. Anna was too big to get more than her nose under the bed, but that she did, snuffling and growling excitedly, the whole back end of her quivering. Unc pulled out the bed, walked around and reached into the corner. Between two fingers, he held up a slender, squirming creature. "Martin's little garter snake!" he announced. In the meantime, across the hall, the twins slept like kingdom come.

"That Martin!" exclaimed Unc. He couldn't help laughing. Thad chuckled. Anna circled Unc and the snake. Evvie, usually so composed and sensible, now felt foolish.

Unc handed the snake to Thad. He rolled the bed in place and settled the girls on their pillows. "Go to sleep, chicks," he murmured fondly, and patted them.

Evvie snuggled close to Lizette. "It was never a dragon, you know," she whispered, "and it was silly of me to be so scared."

The summer night swept into the room on cool wings. It brought gifts to the sisters—a whisper of leaves, a twinkle of stars, the promise of tomorrow—sleep.

6.

Mush for Supper

IN THE morning Unc received a long distance phone call from his business partner in Torbridge. After the conversation he seemed troubled. "Kids," he announced, "I'm obliged to leave you. Your parents promised to return by supper-time this evening. Surely you will be all right until then."

"Of course," snapped Martin. "I don't see why you think we're babies." He flashed an injured look at Unc. "It isn't every day a guy finds a really good snake." Martin had heard from his sisters how the snake had strayed from his room into theirs, and how Unc or Thad Conroy had turned it loose in the grass.

"Indeed we're not babies, Unc," declared Lizette. "We're almost twelve and we're ten and nine." To be without grownups for a whole day would be exciting, now that it was broad daylight.

"You won't starve," reasoned Unc. "I'll run over and explain to Mrs. Van Winkle. She's too fat to do much walking, but she'll keep an eye on you from a distance." Unc fussed around like a mother hen. When he departed, suit-case in hand, to take the trolley-car for Torbridge, he gave final advice. "You'll be good, won't you, and not get into mischief?"

The girls looked as sweet as angel cake. The boys grinned. They said they would be good like pirates and outlaws and wild Indians, and it would be a day of days! But when Unc forced himself to say good-bye, Max and Martin whispered they would faithfully look after house, land, and sisters, and none should come to harm. It was too bad, though, about that snake, and hadn't Unc ever been a boy? "Not twin boys," answered Unc, and went off, feeling nervous.

As he disappeared up the street, Lizette said they might as well begin playing. "Let's play favorite colors. Mine is pink. When I'm grown up and rich, I shall have everything pink—wallpaper, carpets, curtains, party dresses and hats—pink—" Lizette paused, quite overcome with charming visions.

"I s'pose you'll have pink knobs on your doors," jeered Max.

"Bet you'll have the pink-eye, too," taunted Martin.

"Let's tell our favorite flowers," suggested Evvie, kindly changing the game. "Mine are lilacs, or else plum blossoms."

"Ours are skunk cabbage," declared Martin. He and Max laughed so like hyenas no one heard Lizette's preference for pink roses.

"Let's tell our favorite food," piped Max, in a high, little-girl voice. "Ours are fat green caterpillars broiled on toast. *Yummy!*" He and Martin rolled off the step and lay on the brick terrace, writhing with glee.

Although such horrid talk threatened to turn their stomachs, Evvie and Lizette couldn't help laughing. But Evvie decided it was time to call a halt on foolishness. "I must set the table for supper," she announced. "Lizette, you could pick pansies for a centerpiece." She peeped into the ice-box. "There's cold roast beef, cottage cheese, apple sauce and custard. Remember how starved we were the day we moved from Fairland? It's a long way. Mamma and Papa and Addy Newton will be as hungry as bears. We really ought to have something nice and hot, instead of cold things."

"Corn meal mush." Max decided it without a moment's hesitation.

"Mush! The folks will be tickled pink!" exclaimed Martin. "And what's left can be fried for breakfast tomorrow, with sausage and maple syrup."

"Mush is awf'ly easy to cook," said Evvie. "We need water in a kettle and the mush-paddle for stirring. Corn meal, too."

"Then what are we waiting for?" asked Max. He dashed to the cupboard, flung open the lower doors, and with a great banging, dragged out the iron pot. It could look back on a long career of mush-making.

"We'll build the fire for you," shouted Martin.

"It's too early," Evvie decided. She and Lizette, thinking that Addy Newton might have an eagle eye, dusted where it showed. They gathered bouquets, while the boys hung about, impatient for the cooking of mush.

At last Evvie gave the word. Expertly the twins closed the dampers of *Old Home Comfort*. They lifted the lids over the firebox, stuffed paper and kindling through the holes, struck at least ten matches simply for the joy of it, and as the kindling caught, laid the axe-hewn sticks. Such a fragrance of burning wood, of clean wood smoke! Max opened the dampers. The fire soon settled down to a steady purr.

Lizette ran for the paddle. For two generations it had been dedicated to stirring mush. It was turned over to Evvie. "We don't need much water," she declared, peering into the black cavern of the kettle. Handmaiden Lizette stood by, holding a big pan of meal braced firmly against her stomach. Evvie dipped into the pan, sifting the meal into the water through her fingers. The powdery grains sank dismally to the bottom.

"You have to stir all the time," advised Martin.

"Don't I know it?" cried Evvie, splashing for dear life.

"*Shoot*, that's not nearly enough meal," warned Max. "I could put such a little bit of mush in one back tooth and never even taste it! Remember there's six of us and there's Addy Newton. Evvie, put in twice as much. The most important thing about mush is having it to fry for breakfast."

This was certainly true. Lizette refilled the pan. Again, and yet again, Evvie dipped and stirred. The water was beginning to steam. The meal was rising through it in a promising cloud. How wonderfully capable the young Hudsons felt. Mush for supper—delicious mush!

Suddenly, without warning, the cloudy liquid in the pot did indeed become mush. It thickened to a stiff paste. The paddle wouldn't budge. "Water!" screamed Evvie. "More water!"

Martin leaped to the sink and grabbed a tin basin. Filling it hurriedly from the tap, he ran back and dumped the water into the kettle. Alas, it would have been impossible for the most promising mush to withstand such an icy shock. It stiffened into marble. It died. Craters and crevasses and lakes formed on its waxy surface.

"Now see what you've done!" stormed Evvie.

Martin looked so stricken that she added, "*Fiddle,* it's my fault! I remember now it should've been *boiling* water. The meal should've been mixed with *cold* water and stirred in a little at a time."

So Evvie filled the teakettle and placed it on the stove in case of need. The fire was replenished. Four round heads bent over the pot, anxiously watching. As the mixture re-heated, Evvie and the twins took turns with the paddle, digging, struggling, stirring like fury.

Before long the lumpy pulp was bubbling—*plup, plop*—as thickly as lava in a volcanic crater. "Great Scott, it's growing!" shouted Max, frantically. "Look alive, Evvie, it's about to run over the sides!"

The moment was crucial. Evvie, her cheeks as red as her hair, rushed for a large aluminum kettle. Feverishly she began spooning into it from the pot. White blobs dripped and sizzled on the red-hot stove. "More water!" panted Evvie.

"We put in too much corn meal, I betcha," observed Max.

"You were the one, Mister, who said we wouldn't even have enough mush for your back tooth." Evvie was bitter.

So now there were two kettles of mush to stir. Again the meal swelled and swelled. And just as a third, and then a fourth container was brought to the rescue and filled, there came the sound of wheels in the lane.

All but Evvie, faithfully toiling and moiling, deserted the mush and scampered out the kitchen door. Their joyous shouts came back to her. "It's Papa and Mamma! They're home! They've got a cow hitched to the back of the surrey!"

Evvie's glance darted wildly from the spattered stove to the dusty tracks on the floor, from the four streaked kettles to their awful contents. She gulped down a sob. Fiercely she snatched a broom and swept a thick sprinkling of meal into a corner. Wearily she heard Mamma's voice. "Where is our Evvie?"

"She's—we're cooking mush for your supper," answered Lizette, skipping happily. How like Lizette not to realize that the mush-making had turned out to be drudgery! And to tell first thing, too!

Mamma and the other children entered the stifling kitchen. Papa, carrying the suit-case, brought up the rear. In a single glance Mamma saw everything—the dusty floor, the hot stove thronged with smeared pots, discouraged Evvie gamely trying to muster a smile.

"Darling," said Mamma, taking Evvie's fiery cheeks between her cool hands. She turned her head to look at Papa, saying all in a breath, "Isn't it lovely, John, having mush for supper?"

"Mamma, I just noticed!" squealed Lizette. "Where is Addy Newton? Didn't she come to do all the work and wash the dishes 'n everything?"

"We'll explain later," said Papa, quietly. He looked a little grim. But Mamma was bright and smiling. "First we'll have supper," she said.

The roast beef slices were thin and delicate. The gelatine salad melted fruitily on the tongue. The apple sauce smoothed thick and tart on buttered bread. And of course there was MUSH!

"I guess I forgot to salt it," murmured Evvie, taking a troubled sip from her spoon. "I'm afraid there are lots of lumps." Her lips trembled.

"Aw, salt!" scorned Max. "Who likes salt, anyway?"

"Nobody but cows and sheep," declared Martin. "As for lumps, I love 'em. They make mush seem lots more'n it really is." Martin looked at Evvie with sincerest admiration.

"Evvie can cook," boasted Lizette. "But we all helped," she added, anxious not to be left out.

"The mush is delicious, children." Papa was chewing underdone lumps with brave relish.

Mamma looked around the table, smiling. "Bless kindness," she said softly.

7.

From Cellar to Cupola

AFTER supper Papa explained about Addy Newton. "On the way to Fairland your mamma said firmly that she intended to get along without hired help. I pled and I argued," confessed Papa, making a funny little face at Mamma, "but all in vain."

Mamma laughed and tossed her head. "We can't afford Addy just now," she said, lightly. "I have two strong sons and two spry daughters. If four pairs of hands are not enough to help me do the work of this house, there's something the matter with the hands and minds of the children who own them. We shall all work together, and not mind it. You can milk the cow and harness the horses and mow the lawns and run errands. Both boys and girls can wash and wipe dishes. In winter you can shovel snow and help to tend the furnace. Right now Evvie could prepare the whole of a good breakfast if she would set her mind to it. I will teach both my girls to cook. And to mend," added Mamma.

"Mamma! Mending!" cried Lizette, full of dread. "But," she went on, "I shall cook beautiful desserts. I shall cook new fancy dishes—things you never heard of before."

"What, f'r instance?" demanded Martin. "Bet you don't know yourself."

"I'll find them in Mamma's cook-book, and in the newspapers," reasoned Lizette. "I will read them. They will be easy. I'll be the best cook in Fairland—I mean, in Winfield."

"Bravo! A noble ambition!" said Papa.

In spite of his praise, Evvie and the twins giggled. Lizette was always high-flown. She would ever be like the girl in the fairy tale who couldn't open her mouth but that pearls and roses fell out of it.

"Papa, wasn't it kind of ticklish business letting Addy Newton know she was not to come here, after all?" asked Max.

"Yes," answered Papa, "but she was good-natured about it, for I found a place for her in Fairland, where she is to nurse and cook for an aged woman. Later, when I have established a good medical practice in Winfield, we shall have Addy Newton, or someone like her. In the meantime, you are to be as brisk as bees in helping your mother."

"Addy would've been somebody new," murmured Martin, regretfully. "Great Scott, Mamma, dishes are not boys' work! Surely you don't believe that!"

"Dishes are boys' work when it's necessary," Papa put in, firmly. "Children who live in a good home with plenty of food and clothing and love, should do their share in keeping it up. Boys, suppose you and I wash the dishes this very evening."

"All those mush pots!" objected Max. But he laughed in spite of himself.

Papa laughed, too. "We'll clean the kettles while our ladies sit in the parlor and look pretty." Presently Papa and the twins were making a great clatter in the kitchen and howling with laughter. They had a better time than the ladies who took their ease.

Before breakfast the next morning Max and Martin were in the

barn milking the new cow. While the chore was being done, the
girls made friends with the newcomer, stroking her and feeding her
wisps of hay. They talked about a name for her. It was *Biddy* that
Evvie decided upon.

"Now wait a minute," protested Max. "That's a name for a hen,
not a cow."

"Great Scott, yes!" agreed Martin.

But Evvie was the eldest. Her word was often law. Lizette had
held out rather strongly for Rapunzel, who was a story-book princess.
"Because," urged Lizette, "the cow's tail reminds me of Rapunzel's
long, golden braids." The twins laughed so uproariously they almost
upset the milk pail. After such a foolish, far-fetched suggestion, the
name of Biddy seemed altogether right. Evvie giggled, but she slipped
her arm around her little sister, knowing that life sometimes became
confusingly real for such a dreamer.

Breakfast was fried mush, of course. Maple syrup helped to get
it down. The children had hardly finished the dishes when George
Akers appeared at the kitchen door.

"Joy!" breathed Evvie. For George was holding the hand of the
blind girl who lived up Bishop Street. Eagerly Evvie ran to lead the
child into the house. As she took charge, every inch of Evvie Hudson
brimmed with tenderness for Madge Ross. Lizette hung back. The
twins were shy. But George was perfectly natural, and Mamma, as
usual, said the right thing. "How nice of you, George, to bring a new
little girl for all of us to know!"

"It's the nicest thing George ever did in his life!" declared Evvie,
fervently.

"George said you were dandy people, and about my age," explained
Madge, smiling. "I'm eleven and a half."

"Like me," said Evvie, simmering with a deep pleasure.

"George said you would show me the cupola on top of the house,"

Madge went on. "He says it's exciting."

"Tell you what we'll do," offered Max. "Let's begin with the cellar and go straight up. Even George hasn't seen all of our house."

"Evvie, take good care of Madge," whispered Mamma, as the twins led the way. In the cellar George whistled. "*Whew*, it's three times bigger than most cellars."

"It's ours," minced Lizette.

"Some folks talk big, 'specially when they shouldn't," scolded Max.

"I mean—" began Lizette. But Evvie was explaining to Madge that the cellar smells were partly those of stored apples, potatoes, and piles of coal, and that shelves held canned fruits and jellies brought from Fairland.

On the first floor again, Madge glided her hands over the smooth surfaces of the big square piano, over the corner whatnot, the ornaments on its shelves, and those on the mantels, and she "knew" the shapes of chairs and sofas. Her fingers explored with delicate curiosity. Feeling space about her, she could guess the largeness of rooms.

George had little to say, but looked at everything with boyish interest.

"We like this room best of all," said Lizette, the first one to step into the library. She shot a look at Max, in case he believed she was boasting again.

"Sure we do," he agreed. The Hudson children did not explain that here, in honor of their beloved books, the floweriest carpet had been laid, the finest lace curtains hung, the best furniture placed. Here the fruit-like bindings, red, blue, fawn and green bloomed behind polished glass. Evvie opened the doors and guided Madge's fingers along the rows of volumes. The other children, closing their eyes, did likewise, to discover how the books felt to Madge's seeing fingers.

"Madge, if you'd like it, we'll come back here directly and I'll read to you out of our wonderful old bound *St. Nicholas*." Evvie opened the cupboards below the shelves, revealing the magazines. She threw a family-secret look toward Lizette and the twins. "Shall we tell Madge and George?" she asked.

Answering nods gave Evvie leave. Eyes glowing, she drew three magazines from the hoard. "In these," she explained, "are three stories written by our father, John Hudson. He wrote them when he was young and had to pay his own way through medical school. We think Papa's stories are wonderful. You see how we've read the magazines almost to rags. It seems queer and marvelous that Papa was ever a real author. He thinks it's queer, too. He laughs and turns red when we dare to mention it."

"It all happened before Evvie and the twins and I were ever living on this earth," Lizette explained further.

"And look at us now!" Max grinned and struck himself on the chest.

"Large as life and twice as sassy," joked Martin. The children ran into the hall and trooped up the stairs, their laughter dancing around them like fly-away fiddle notes.

In the eight upper bedrooms the guests were shown special treasures. Madge studied Lizette's dolls, and those belonging to Evvie, now sacredly kept but no longer played with. To the twins Madge was simply great because she didn't shiver as she fingered the bones in their collection, and were told that this or that was part of dog, frog, mole or woodchuck.

Presently eager young feet were storming the ladder to the cupola. "Wish my folks had a cupalow," yearned George. Madge felt her way around—window-panes, window-seats. She was told of the view over the treetops. She felt the heat of the sun in the narrow confines of the dome. She felt the pleasure and the nearness of the other children. Her face was radiant.

"It is like a fairy tower," gushed Lizette. "Little did I dream when

I was born, Madge, that I would ever live in a house with a cupola. Oh, Madge, if you could only *really* see it!"

"Lizette!" scolded Evvie. "Madge can see better than any of us, because she sees with her *soul!* If you are going to talk that way to her, I wish you would go and do something else."

Lizette felt stricken. Not for the world would she have hurt Madge. She felt a rush of burning anger at Evvie. Hadn't she made Lizette's slip of the tongue far worse?

The boys paid little attention to the spat. They were now absorbed in Max's burning-glass. It was his most wonder-working possession. He loved to experiment with it. He had slipped it out of its little case, and focused it on an inch of window-seat. Soon a blinding bright spot flickered under the glass. Its edges began to smolder. Hastily

Max smudged out the burn with his thumb.

"C'mon, let's all go to the pond," suggested Martin. As the children clattered down the stairs, the memento of their visit to the cupola was a small, black-rimmed hole in the leather cover of the seat. From the barnyard they looked back. The windows of the dome were a-gleam with reflections of sun and shining morning clouds. "Cupola House!" murmured Evvie, fondly.

"The cupola is like a glass hat up there." For once Max showed a fancy almost as airy as Lizette's. She laughed in delight. Then she remembered how boiling mad she was at Evvie. Just look at her now, behaving as if she had discovered Madge Ross, or that she had been appointed by some lordly authority to be Madge's one and only friend and guide! *I wish you would go off and do something else,* Evvie had said to Lizette.

Lizette *would* go. But it was hard. How she longed to show Madge the green tunnel of the grape-arbor, the flower and vegetable gardens, the big barn, the pond, and Sir Dragor's grave and headstone! Yes, and afterward, in the cool, quiet library, how well Lizette could read to Madge out of *St. Nicholas!* But Lizette wasn't wanted, at least by Evvie. Oh, well, she was always welcome at the woodcutter's peaceful cottage. Head down, Lizette turned and ran.

"Sister!" called Evvie. Her voice held a pleading note. But Lizette paid no attention.

8.

A Very Hot Day

"THIS is good weather for taking things easy," remarked Mrs. Van Winkle. "We'll just set and rock and fan ourselves." She allowed Lizette to read what she had recorded in her diary the day before. She had no secrets.

In Cool of morning worked with my flowers, read Lizette. *The Queen of the Prerry Rose is in bloom agen. Made bred. Doc Hudson and the missus come back from Fairland with a new cow. P.D. and I had roasten ears and Blackberry pie for dinner. P.D. had collic. King edward of England has been sick. He is better. After dinner I cleaned the Organ and red up the Parlor. Between times I kep an eye on the Hudson Children. Filled my Fountain pen.*

Lizette thought the diary was thrilling. "Madge Ross is over at our house," she said. "Do you know her?"

A tender look overspread Mrs. Van's face. "Madge and I are friends," she answered. "Sometimes she comes to see me and my flowers. She touches them, light as air. She smells 'em. I s'pect that flowers make her as happy as anything in life, same as they do me."

Lizette walked to the back entry. She could see Evvie and Madge strolling hand in hand toward Sir Dragor's grave. Then they hadn't

51

gone to the pond with the boys. Evvie was all shining attention for the blind child. She was looking as happy as only a willingly helpful person can look. Lizette dragged her feet as she returned to Mrs. Van Winkle's sitting room. "I could read to you," she suggested, her voice lonely.

Lizette selected a story about a girl named Cora. A fairy took Cora on a long journey to show her how people all over the world were working. Cora caught on, crying at last, "Oh, Fairy Workall, I see that everyone is busy except myself. I will truly try in the future to be a help to someone."

Lizette was relieved when she found this to be only a dream of Cora's, for she had begun to feel that she and Cora were unpleasantly alike—useless. Papa had sometimes hinted it. She had no more than read how Cora became an entirely different and much better person, when she was startled by the most frightful din she had ever heard. It came from afar, yet it seemed heart-shakingly near, an eerie, repeated caterwauling beginning with a deep moan, and whining upward to a piercing scream.

"It's the fire whistle," remarked Mrs. Van Winkle. She stopped rocking and turned her gaze toward the town. Lizette's book dropped to the floor as her hands went up over her ears. In Fairland when fire was discovered the bells of the village churches were rung. That was bad enough, but nothing like this fearful alarm. Lizette began to tremble as her ready fancy formed terrible pictures. She crept over to stand within the comforting circle of Mrs. Van's arm. "There, there!" soothed her friend. "The engines will soon outen the fire, wherever it is."

But even as she gave comfort, her nose sniffed the air. "Smells near-by," she decided. She rose from her chair, and followed closely by Lizette, called out of the kitchen door. "P.D., do you smell smoke?" The head and shoulders of P.D. appeared above the garden bushes, where he was working. But Mrs. Van did not wait for the rest of him. For now came another and more varied clamor. Hurrying through the house and out to the front porch, she and Lizette saw what was rushing toward them on Bishop Street.

It was the fire engine, a streak of scarlet and gleaming brass, manned by men in helmets and red shirts. Smoke, spangled with fiery sparks, poured from the engine's funnel. The bell was madly a-swing— *clang, clang, clang.* The driver was braced tensely, arms and reins taut. Under his management, two splendid grays plunged at breakneck gallop, their hoofs thundering, ears back, nostrils distended, every great muscle at work. Behind them came the hook-and-ladder wagon at full tilt, drawn by a pair of blacks as swift and powerful as the grays. There was an earth-shaking rumble of wheels, a rattle of heavy metal. Preceding the entire frenzied procession sped a spotted coach dog, barking furiously. Behind the hook-and-ladder wagon came Dr. John Hudson, his cart careening from side to side, and Molly the mare wildly shying and plunging. The procession crashed across the Hudsons' south lawn without grazing a single tree. The steeds halted, tossing their proud heads. The coach dog leaped into the seat quickly vacated by the driver and sat back on his haunches, as if to say, "There, I did it again!"

The hose was unreeled and one end dropped into the outside cistern. There was a storm of hoarse shouts, a clang of metal as the ladders were lifted to the roof of the Hudson house.

For the cupola, which the children had visited less than two hours ago, was now a cage of flame, alive and leaping!

For a moment Lizette was too stunned to move. Then, her throat full of small, gasping cries, she jumped from the porch. She left the Van Winkles' picket gate swinging wide as she ran to join Mamma under the elm tree. All of the family were there except Papa, who was in the thick of the fight. Neighbors were carrying furniture out.

Chairs, sofas, tables, vases, lamps and dishes appeared on the lawn as lost and purposeless as a jumble of orphans having no place to go and no one to love them.

"It is Papa's orders that we stay here together, so he will know exactly where we are," said Mamma. "So you are not to stir a step. George, take Madge home. Be very careful of her amid this crowd." Mamma's voice was quiet, but her face was as white as her collar. Her hands trembled on the children's shoulders. Once Papa hastened up, trying to give comfort. In that moment, while no one seemed to be looking, Max slipped away.

Maxwell Hudson was probably the most wretched boy in the world. Not fifteen minutes ago he and Martin and George had been playing happily at the pond. And then— "Listen to that fire whistle!" George had cried. "C'mon, fellas, let's go." Full of excitement, the boys had run along the pasture lane. At the barnyard gate they had halted, thunderstruck, to see above the trees the burning cupola. Cheeks prickling, eyes popping, they had torn across the yard just as the fire trucks appeared in the leafy distance of Bishop Street.

Now, staring horror-stricken at the flames, Max suddenly felt as if he had been struck a hard blow over the heart. Could it be possible that he, Max Hudson, had—*no, NO!* . . . *Yes?* Oh, then he would run away! Away from everyone, away from himself, far away. The muscles of his legs twitched with the desire to take to his heels. Yet he had never loved or needed his family so much. There seemed also to be a terrible weight in his right-hand pocket.

Max stole another look at his mother, white and grief-stricken. He saw his sisters, trembling and crying. He saw his twin, struggling against tears. He saw Papa carrying books from the library. It was then he scuttled around the other side of the house, in at the front door, and up the stairs. In his mother's room he snatched an object from the wall. It was an oval-framed portrait of her father.

Clasping the photograph, Max heard the crash of axes on the roof. He smelled the terrible burning. The cupola—*Cupola House!* Max picked up Mamma's pillow from her bed. Crushing it against his face, he spilled into it a great sob. It was a sob that left its print on the snowy casing—the print of a boy's cheeks and fingers, mud-stained from his morning play.

There was another terrible crash above him. Full of panic, he ran into the upper hall and saw through an open door the room he shared with Martin. "Our collections!" he moaned. He darted into the room. There they were, in mortal danger—the birds' nests, the stamps and scrap books, the hair ribbons stolen from Fairland girls, the rocks and marbles, the school pennants, the locust shells and bottled spiders, the treasured bones, lovingly scraped, washed and polished.

Carrying a bone and the photograph, Max returned to his family. "Son!" cried Mamma. "I just now missed you. Where have you been?"

Max thrust the photograph into Mamma's hands. "I saved it for you," he blurted out. "Here!" he added, handing the bone to his twin.

Mamma looked at the picture, and at Max, so awkward and pale. Her face worked, and for the first time, she gave way to weeping. Now even Martin cried. But Max's grief was too deep for tears.

"None of that crying," chided Papa, coming up. "The Chief declares the fire to be under control. It's only a matter of minutes, now, until it is put out."

Every face brightened. The house was safe. Yet no one could feel very happy. For alas, the cupola, the fairy tower, the sparkling glass hat was gone forever. There were also the broken, melted roof slates, the smoking rafters. Papa said there would be need of plastering and painting and papering in the upper bedrooms. His mouth was grim. Mamma looked very troubled. The expense, just after buying the house!

Neighbors helped to carry things back to their places. Mamma served the firemen coffee and cakes. The coach dog showed off his tricks. Soon firemen, horses, trucks, dog and townsfolk were gone. Mrs. Van Winkle called over the picket gate, inviting the Hudsons to a noon meal.

"The coffee will do the doctor and me," answered Mamma, "but

I would be grateful if you would feed the children."

It made the young Hudsons feel homesick to leave Papa and Mamma, when everyone was feeling so sad and worn-out. Yet the prospect of hot food seemed inviting. The Van Winkle table was set in a sunny bay. It was Mrs. Van's habit to dine from a rocking chair, which seemed odd, but comfortable. Mr. Van wore his hat. He had his private reasons for always doing so. He said not more than three words, but kindness was in every placid motion, in every generous offering.

"Never saw a boy eat so pindlin'," fretted Mrs. Van, studying Max.

"I don't like our house without the cupola," moaned Lizette into her glass of milk.

Max got up suddenly, murmured an excuse and stumbled hastily out of the house. Everyone looked a bit startled. Martin turned red. He knew what ailed Max as well as if he himself had been the one to —Martin squirmed, refusing second helpings. He was glad when the meal was over.

The Hudsons worked hard that afternoon. By supper-time Uncle Greg had arrived. Evvie snuggled sadly up to him. "Now we can't call it *Cupola House* anymore," she grieved.

"I'm tired of hearing that," growled Martin. He was worn out with his silent imaginative sharing of Max's torment.

"When I can afford it, I'm going to have another cupola built," announced Papa.

"Goody!" squealed the children. Even Max's heart lifted, but he could say nothing.

"It will be expensive," Unc objected. "When the roof is repaired, you had better leave it off. I liked it myself, but after all, it was only an ornament."

"Edith and I have been talking it over," said Papa. "Ornament or not, we have decided it's not fair to the handsome old house not to replace it. I think we should always be sorry."

"We'll pinch and do without, in order to build a new cupola," said Mamma. "Martin, bring the Hunter County atlas. It has an engraving of this house, made when it was first built."

The children were astonished. To Lizette and Evvie, at least, the atlas had been useful only as a home for paper dolls. "See," said Papa, "the cupola in the picture, lightning rods and all, will serve as a model for the carpenters." Papa closed the big book. "And now," he went on, "I understand that you children were in the cupola this morning. Could anything have happened then to start the fire? Evvie? Lizette?"

"We were just showing Madge and George around," answered Evvie.

"We didn't do anything bad," testified Lizette.

"Martin?" Papa asked.

Martin's eyes flickered and glazed over. He had no more expression than a fish.

"Max, then? Son, will you empty out your pockets?"

With a trembling hand, Max piled his clutter on the table. There was a wad of string, his pen-knife, three marbles, five nails and two screws. There was an inch of peppermint stick, one licorice baby, five rusty keys on a ring, a small whetstone and a pencil stub. There was a burning-glass in a neat case.

"I'll take the glass, Max," said Papa.

Max let out a tight, shaking breath. "I remember burning a little hole in the window-seat," he confessed. "But I smudged it out. I mean I thought I did. Papa," choked Max, "I was as proud of the cupola as anyone. I wouldn't have set it on fire for—for a million dollars!"

"Of course not," answered Papa. "I've seen how tormented you've been all day. You've been thinking how your careless play with the burning-glass might have destroyed this house and everything in it. Perhaps *somebody* in it. You deserve punishment, Max. I'll let you choose what it will be."

Max felt that nothing could be too severe. He rolled his eyes at his father. "Don't let me build us a boat for the pond," he croaked.

Papa blinked. "But that would also be punishing Marty," he reasoned, presently. "Marty was planning to share the boat-building with you."

Martin gulped down his farewell to the boat. "Great Scott, Papa," he mumbled, "if Max can do without it, I can, too."

9.

Gentle Horse

"MARTY and I could sell some of the watermelons," suggested Max. "We'd make money to build a new cupola." The merest mention of the fire was difficult for Max. The weight of guilt would be on him for a long time. But the family had been kind, agreeing that of course Max didn't do wrong intentionally.

"There are lots of ripe pears, too." Martin was fired with enthusiasm. "*Jiminy*, we could go up Bishop Street, both sides, and sell at every house!"

"You couldn't make enough money to build a new cupola, of course," Mamma explained. "But your earnings might pay for the school supplies we shall be buying next month. Every little saving will help Papa, now. Don't build up your hopes too much. Many people up the street have small garden plots of their own. I'll telephone Papa at his office and see what he thinks of this selling venture."

Unc was staying over a day or two. He was helping Mr. Van Winkle lay boards over the damaged sections, and spreading and anchoring a vast sheet of tarpaulin. On the ladder going up, Unc turned to make a remark which sank deep with Lizette. "I can just see a physician's children going from door to door, selling. Heavens, the town of Winfield will believe them to be on the verge of starvation!"

Mamma reported to Papa by telephone. "Nonsense!" laughed Papa. "Thanks to the Warrens, who owned the place before us, there are plenty of fruits and vegetables. The selling experience will be good for the youngsters. Tell Max I approve. We'll talk it over when I come home."

The whole family, plus George Akers, even Unc, gathered pears, beans and corn that evening. Mamma said she could spare cucumbers and peppers. There were tomatoes.

The twins laid plans for hauling the produce in the pair of wagons they had owned since they were six. They tossed off any suggestion of hard labor. "We'll just have to make a lot of trips back and forth," they declared, stoutly.

Mamma said that would take a tiresome long time. "It might seem odd to sell from the family surrey," she said, "but I see nothing against it. You could take orders for the melons, and return with them in your wagons."

"I'll drive Silas," offered Evvie, eagerly. "I'll hold the reins and guard the vegetables while the boys knock on people's doors." Both Evvie and Mamma often drove Silas. He was gentle, even poky. The family trusted him.

Lizette listened to the plans. They sounded exciting. She wasn't sure she wanted to go, yet she could well be the lucky one to sit in the surrey and hold the pint jar Max was readying. Lizette would bring it home full of money for the purchase of pencils, paper and school books.

The next morning Silas was hitched to the surrey. The baskets of fruit and vegetables were placed on the floor below the back seat. Evvie lifted the reins. Beside her sat the twins. George took his place on the back seat amid piles of unshucked roasting ears. "C'mon, Lizette, sit by me," he urged.

Lizette had brushed her curls with unusual care, in case she decided to go. Now she looked at Unc, who appeared disapproving. She remembered what he had said last evening. "I'm not going, George," answered Lizette. No one on Bishop Street was going to look at Lizette this morning as if she were a poor little match-girl. Oh my, no! Whatever the townspeople were to say about the other Hudsons, Lizette would not be included. She would stay at home in pride and dignity—a lady.

Within a few minutes after the departure of the surrey, Mamma had Lady Lizette drying dishes. She had to dust the sitting-room, always a chore because of the piano. She had to do a bit of sewing and use a thimble, which she hated. How far had the children gone by now? Were the twins collecting many dimes and nickels in the pint jar?

Lizette took her last crooked stitch. She ran across the lane to the Van Winkle cottage. "They're all gone," she announced, her eyes solemn. "They've gone up Bishop Street to sell pears and beans and things to buy lumber and glass for a new cupola."

"Well, now," exclaimed the plump neighbor, "that's a spunky thing to do! It will be something different to write in my day book. The children will have lots of fun, and the Bishop Street folk glad to have fresh garden sass."

"I was invited to go." Lizette was anxious to say it. "But my uncle said—I mean there might've been worms in the roasting ears on the back seat that would crawl out on me."

"Go get one of my fresh cookies out of the jar," advised Mrs. Van. "Child, be sure you have more fun than fear in this life." It sounded like scolding, however gentle.

So Lizette said thanks and walked home, thoughtfully munching her cooky. She seated herself on the front steps, gazing up Bishop Street. "More fun than fear"—*oh, shoot the luck!* She sat there, feeling sorry she was not in the surrey, blaming herself for being—well, for being Lizette Hudson. She'd make up for it when she was older. Then she'd be perfect. She would do great things. Everybody would be completely surprised. For one thing, she would write books. She had known it for a long time, but if she had mentioned it, Max and Martin, and even Evvie, would say it was one of her overblown fancies. Lizette began enjoying herself with dreams of future fame. Talk about pearls and roses! Why, they would drip from Lizette's pen! And suddenly she had such a wonderful idea she almost fell off the step.

In the meantime the twins were padding around to back doors, as befitted the sale of humble vegetables. They explained, "We're Max and Martin Hudson. We live at the end of the street where the Warrens used to live."

"Oh, yes, where the roof burned yesterday. How is your mother today, after such a fright? Why, the house might have burned to the ground. By-the-way, how does it feel to be a twin? One would need to study you a long time to tell you apart. How did the fire start?"

"It was hot up there in the cupola," answered Martin, saving his twin. He went on. "The Warrens planted a big garden in the spring. We kids are selling part of the crop to help build us a new cupola."

The housewives liked the boys' frankness, and they liked the boys themselves, so clear-eyed and practical. They came out to the surrey to snap the beans and peel back the corn husks. They saw George, whom they knew, and they met the pink-cheeked girl with the red braids. "This is our sister Evvie," said the twins.

"Evalina," Evvie corrected patiently.

The juicy little russet pears began selling briskly. The piles of corn, beans and peppers dwindled. The cucumbers and tomatoes went more slowly. The twins relayed orders for melons to George, who was acting as recording clerk. Moistening his pencil, George scrawled names and locations. *Mis Field with ceeders in yard; Smith with baywinda; Dorans have black cat and kittens; Adams, baby in pen; Ross where Madge lives.* Such items as the cedars and the kittens were to help Max and Martin when they returned to deliver the watermelons.

Madge had been delighted when the Hudsons arrived. She begged her mother to permit her to go on the selling tour. Mrs. Ross was considering it when something happened.

Across the street from the Ross home, dog Anna lay on a front porch, letting on that it was she, rather than Merchant Conroy, who owned the house, the lot, and the Conroy family. Ears up, Anna gazed at the group around the Hudson surrey. She listened to the chatter of voices. Presently she got up and trotted across the pavement. Hugely she planted herself under the nose of the old horse.

Silas had never seen Anna. Was she a dog? She smelled like one. But she was the size of a calf or colt. Silas sniffed, and took a restless step away from Anna. "Whoa," said Evvie, tightening the reins a little. But she was not uneasy. She knew Silas well, the poky old thing.

Or did she? For at that moment Anna lifted her head and barked. It was the bark of a great Dane, hoarse, deep and resounding. Silas reared up in terror. He plunged forward, frantic to get away from the strange animal. For a moment the reins fell slack in Evvie's hands as she was thrown against the dashboard. But she jerked herself upright, tugging on the bit, calling shrilly to the horse. Madge's mother had jumped away from the wheels, pulling Madge with her. George just saved himself from falling out, his hand flying to grasp support. The twins, at first so startled as to become stone images, came to attention. They sped after the lurching surrey.

It was Max who reached Silas first. Running his hand along the shaft, he leaped forward to catch the left curb rein. There he hung with desperate determination, although tossed by the strong plunging motions of the horse. People burst from their houses with shouts of *whoa*. Two elderly men risked life and limb by planting themselves in Silas's path and waving their arms. Silas only swerved dangerously.

Suddenly there was Thad Conroy. He was young and long-legged. Cuffing Anna out of the way, he ran up beside Silas. Now, with both Thad and Max hanging to his bridle, and Evvie tugging on the reins with all her strength, the bit in the horse's mouth was painful. He slowed, then halted, trembling and subdued as Thad stroked him and spoke soothing words. Max dropped to his feet, shaky and pale. Evvie relaxed, wrists and arms aching.

At first no one could say a word. But when they looked at one another; when they thought how surprising it was that gentle old Silas had turned into a wild runaway steed; when they saw the vegetables spilled and mixed together; when they realized no one was seriously hurt, they doubled up with laughter. George made the situation funnier when he said, "D'you know something, Thad? Every time I'm with the Hudson kids, something happens. Yesterday it was a fire. Today it's the runaway. I wasn't acshally there when Martin nearly rolled off the roof, but I might've been."

Before leaving the children, Thad helped them to sort and re-assemble the vegetables. George and the twins ran around, plucking from the pavement a bean or an ear of corn, a split tomato, a dusty pepper. "Gee whiz, looky!" cried Martin, retrieving the Mason jar. It was cracked, but the lid was on tight. The coins were safe.

At home once more, the children rattled off the tale of the morning's adventure. Mamma gasped and stepped to the door to take an astonished look at Silas. Unc hurried out to examine shafts and wheels. The twins had sold almost all of the produce. Breathlessly the money was counted. Over six dollars! It was riches! What a wonderful morning, now that it was safely over! The children gazed at Lizette with pity. But she tossed her head, saying, "Who wants to be in a runaway?"

"It was exciting," declared Evvie, forgetting how frightened she had been.

The twins, tired as they were, lifted melons into their wagons. To fill orders, they must make more than one trip, although George went home and brought his own wagon. "The melons will bring us forty cents apiece," crowed Max. And as the three boys trudged up the street, he said, "Before we started out this morning I vowed to myself I'd sell everything or bust. On account of the cupola, you know. And we pretty near did bust up."

At the supper table the children were still elated over the money they had made. Papa praised them. He said he would start a cupola fund. "What else can we do to make money?" mused Max.

"Children cannot be earners to any great extent," Mamma pointed out. "One good way is to do without things."

The children looked gloomy. Doing without seemed undramatic, indeed.

"Someday I shall make piles of money for all of us," announced Lizette.

"How?" inquired Evvie.

"I am going to write a book."

"What about? Fairies? Your never-never land?" Martin snickered a little.

"No," answered Lizette. "Today, when I was sitting on the front steps waiting for you to come back in the surrey, I made up my mind. I'm going to write the story of Tig that Papa has told us so often. He hasn't time, so I shall do it. Everybody will buy it and like it." Lizette was so earnest and her face so bright that all were impressed. At least they pretended to be, for Lizette's sake.

"What Lizette says might come true," declared Papa, humoring her.

"Lizette's awfully good in spelling and composition. She's only nine. But she's read things like *Jane Eyre* and *When Knighthood Was In Flower* and our bound volumes of *Harper's Magazine*." How good of Evvie to say it!

"Lizette's got a big imagination, you bet," Martin added generously.

"If it were possible, one of us should indeed write the story of Tig someday," said Mamma. "It would make a wonderful book."

"But we can't wait for Lizette to be old enough to do it," argued Max, tossing aside the whole idea. "We need the money for a new cupola right away. I'll never feel right until I see it on top of the house."

10.

"Surprise Cake"

EVVIE had not forgotten Mamma's sacrifice of Addy Newton's help. She became more conscious of the housekeeping. She remembered that Mamma had said she could prepare the family breakfasts once she put her mind to it.

So Evvie began rising early, running down to the kitchen, which was quiet and cool of an August morning. Forehead creased and mouth sober, Evvie set to work. She had already had some experience as a helper. Working alone made her feel more responsible. Naturally apt and practical, she found it not very difficult to fry bacon, to cook eggs in various ways, and to make toast. For a defeated week her coffee was either as pale as tea or it was thick and muddy. Once it turned successful, Evvie began experimenting with baking powder biscuits. When the first ones were served, Max and Martin pretended they were chewing rocks. They vowed they would use the biscuits for building a fence, or in battle with George Akers and some other guys. Evvie turned red, and for a moment her temper smoldered. But then she laughed. In time her biscuits became as light as feathers.

Lizette kept declaring she would soon be making those kingly cakes and queenly puddings she had promised. "We're waiting," teased Martin.

"Great Scott, we'll wait about ten years," giggled Max.

Mornings were busy for everyone. Besides the household chores, the last of the garden produce must be gathered. The house was full of the spicy smell of canning and pickling. But of afternoons there was always some time for play. Lizette invented a new game, which she called "Castle." It was not a castle built of stones, but of airy imaginings. In Lizette's mind it rose grandly from a small natural terrace, towers and bastion, surrounded by a moat. Sir Dragor's grave, near by, lent atmosphere. Evvie was Lord Evelyn. Lizette was his lady. Within the castle two packing boxes served as thrones. Lady Lizette generally stayed put, while her lord rode out on his charger to hunt and fight, bringing home game and trophies. Sometimes, however, the lady rode gently through the leafy park on her noble white steed, warily skirting the myrtle bed where the giant lived.

What part could Madge play in Castle? Lizette decided she should be a marble vase adorning the castle entrance. "Vasey" became her name. She was entranced. Motionless and smiling, she became the best vase possible. She held real flowers—zinnias, sunflowers, holly-hocks or August lilies. Flowers were heaven to Vasey, and these hours with the Hudsons the happiest she had ever known. Evvie she adored.

One day the great Dane came trotting down Bishop Street to pay a call. Quite at home, she stretched herself on the cool grass near Vasey. She looked magnificent enough to fit right into the castle picture. As if she knew she were the crowning touch, she fell into a habit of coming often.

Max and Martin didn't care to play Castle. But more than once they rushed up as barbarians, with waving sticks and horrific shouts, to storm the ramparts. Evvie, red braids flying and fists clenched, battled mightily. Lizette fought with tooth and nail. She left scratches. Anna leaped hugely into the fray without taking sides or acting the least unfriendly. All she wanted was plenty of fun and action. Sooner or later she knocked everyone down. Her trumpet barks echoed throughout the Hudsons' fifteen acres. During the battles Vasey would drop her flowers and laugh and scream and clap her hands.

One afternoon, after a hot fight, the children settled on the grass to rest and cool off. Mamma was reading in the sitting room. Lizette went in to see her. "I wish we could have deviled eggs for supper," said Lizette.

"Why don't you fix them yourself?" suggested Mamma. "Wash eight eggs and put them in a pan. Cover with a lid. Boil about twenty minutes. When the eggs have cooled, cut them in two and mash the yolks with a little butter, vinegar, pepper, salt, mustard and a pinch of sugar."

How easy! Lizette's eyes sparkled. While the eggs boiled and the twenty minutes dragged by, she sat on the kitchen steps reading.

For the eggs the minutes flew and for Lizette also, since her book was so enthralling everything else was forgotten. Suddenly there was a loud exploding sound. There followed smaller ones—*pop*, *pop*, *pop*—they kept going on. "What was that?" everyone cried. "Where—"

Lizette guessed. Her book fell from her lap. She rushed to the kitchen. So did everyone else. What a sight! The water in the pan had boiled dry. The lid had blown off. The eight eggs had exploded, every last one of them. Egg shells, yolks and whites were scattered over stove and walls. The ceiling was peppered. It was shocking! But it was also so funny that everyone howled with laughter, even Mamma. After that, the boys called it "the day the devil really got into the deviled eggs."

Lizette resolved to make up for such a failure. The afternoon Mamma attended the meeting of her missionary society seemed a good time. The boys were playing at the pond. Evvie was at the Ross home, visiting Vasey. It was while Lizette was reading *Aunt Samantha at Saratoga* to Mrs. Van Winkle that she had the inspiration. She excused herself, went home, washed her hands and tied on her apron. She leafed through Mamma's cook-book.

In the back, where there had been blank pages, Mamma had written some recipes given her by enthusiastic friends. Here was one—*Surprise Cake*. How suitable! Lizette's cake would indeed be a happy surprise for hungry folk. Sugar, butter, eggs, milk, baking powder, flour—it couldn't possibly fail.

Lizette got out the mixing bowl. She blended the ingredients, beating with such vigor her cheeks shook. By the time she had poured the batter and slipped the pan into the oven, both table and apron were smeared. There was flour on her chin and in her hair. But she wiped up the table and filled the empty bowl with water. She waited, on the spot, for the cake to bake. Above all, it must not scorch. Nor explode!

It came out fragrant, and beautifully golden. True, it hadn't risen. Perhaps being flat was the Surprise Cake's sly way of surprising unsuspecting cooks. Something new and different!

"I was going to make a pie," said Mamma, when she came home and saw the cake.

"Now you don't need to," answered Lizette, sparkling.

The main part of supper was eaten. Lizette hastened to bring in the dessert. "I made it this afternoon," she announced. "It's called *Surprise Cake*."

"Surprise?" echoed Martin. "What's inside? Bugs?"

"It looks like a fine cake," said Papa. "Smells good, too. How wonderful of our Lizette to bake it for us!"

Flushed with pride, Lizette set a knife to the cake. Perhaps she was excited. Perhaps the knife was dull. For cutting the cake was like cutting thick cardboard. "Let me try," offered Papa. He, too, had a hard time. Straining his muscles, however, the slicing was finally done and the pieces served.

Mamma pretended she had an errand to the kitchen. When she returned and found the family still battling with Lizette's cookery, she said, "The cake would have been perfect if Lizette hadn't used corn-starch instead of baking powder. I know, because the can of starch is still on the kitchen table, with the lid off."

So that was the reason the batter had not risen. That was why the cake was as stiff as if it had been starched and ironed. Mamma patted Lizette's shoulder. "Never mind," she soothed, "the same accident might have happened to any new cook."

"The cake is good," Papa repeated firmly.

"It's sweet, and that's what you expect of cake," reasoned Martin, and Evvie nodded in loyal agreement. But then Martin blighted the moment's bloom by saying, "I'm glad my teeth are so strong."

For her own self-respect, Lizette simply had to score a success. A day or two later, with Mamma standing by, she made a pudding. It was a fluffy mixture of cream, eggs and sugar baked in a crust of buttered bread crumbs. It surpassed Lizette's most high-flown aspirations. Now no one could laugh too much about eggs exploding as high as the ceiling, or of starched cake.

All the same, Lizette was no Addy Newton. She was willing to leave cooking alone for a while. There were other things she could do better, although she was not sure just what they were.

11.

"Alice Blue"

OF SEPTEMBER evenings flocks of blackbirds gathered in the maples, making a great flurry and conversation. Lizette read from Mrs. Van's day book. *Divided my pineys and re-set them. Made my Skirt larger around the waste. Picked a bunch of asters for Madge Ross to use in a game she plays at Hudsons.*

There was new stir around the campus. The fall term would soon begin. Madge, who was a professor's daughter, taught the Hudsons the university hymn. She had a pretty voice and could play the piano. The children sang with as much devotion as if they were loyal alumni, or at least members of the senior class. "I shall go to college," vowed Lizette. "After that I shall write my book."

One afternoon the boys hitched Silas to the surrey. Mamma had said to the girls, "Cupola or not, we must have new fall hats. We'll drive to the shop on the Square."

Miss Rupert the milliner was tall and stylish. After one look at Lizette, she said, "Those brown eyes and curls were meant for this brown velvet tam-o'-shanter," as if Lizette was made for the tam, instead of the other way around. Lizette looked at herself in the

mirror. The tam was just right. She loved it. In fact, she quite admired the girl who was wearing it.

An Alice blue tam was selected for Evvie. It set off her blue eyes and red hair. "I'll give you time," she advised her Evvie-image secretly, "for some day you are going to be beautiful. You had just better be."

"Now we'll visit Papa's office," decided Mamma, after paying the milliner. Leaving Silas hitched in the Square, she and the girls were soon climbing the dingy, enclosed stairway. Quietly, in case Papa had some patients, Mamma opened the door. The waiting room was empty, except for Papa himself. He stood at the window, gazing down into the street. There was a dejected droop to his shoulders. Even Lizette could guess that Papa had the blues. Mamma swept across the room and linked her arm in his.

"Well, how nice!" he cried. "I was so deep in thought I didn't hear you come in. It's lucky all my callers are gone. I've had two this afternoon—exactly two!"

"This is not like your crowded office in Fairland," remarked Evvie, before she thought.

"It's only been two months since we came to Winfield," said Mamma, a little sharply. "We can't expect everything to be the same as in Fairland. And this was the only office space we could find in town. It isn't public enough."

"Papa, we have new hats," said Lizette.

"Hooray, let's see them," urged Papa.

The tam-o'-shanters, brown and blue, were displayed. Papa pronounced them *chic*. "Milady," he demanded of Mamma, "where is *your* new hat?"

"Mamma!" wailed Evvie. "I didn't notice! *You* didn't buy a hat for yourself!"

"Why should I?" asked Mamma gaily. "My old one will be new in Winfield."

"Girls," said Papa, "shall we go back to Miss Rupert's and buy Mamma the prettiest hat we can find?"

"Not another word about a hat," vetoed Mamma. And she said to Papa, "John, my dear, for the sake of your spirits, you simply must do something to fill up your idle time. I've been thinking, thinking hard. If you're ready to leave now, let's take a ride in your cart and I'll tell you what's on my mind. Evvie, you and Lizette may go home in the surrey."

Driving Silas along the streets, Evvie was so quiet that Lizette's chatter was silenced. A girl can't talk to a sister who won't say a word.

"Doggone!" muttered Evvie, at last.

"What do you mean?" inquired Lizette.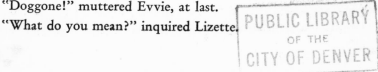

"Nothing," answered Evvie. "But anyway, doggone!"

Papa and Mamma seemed absent-minded that evening. Something was surely simmering. "Anything special around here?" asked Martin.

"Something about the cupola, I bet," ventured Max.

"Such children, noticing and imagining things!" laughed Mamma. She threw Papa a sidelong glance.

The next day would have been ordinary, except that Evvie told Mamma she would like to go upstreet to show Vasey her Alice blue tam. Mamma didn't notice that the fingers of Evvie's right hand were secretly crossed, to put a hex on fibbing.

"It's funny," interrupted Martin, caring nothing about the tam, "you call Madge 'Vasey,' but you blow up because we call you 'Evvie.' "

"Vasey is just a play name. But everyone acts as if Evvie were my really truly born name. *Evvie*"—she spat it out like poison.

"We call you that because we love you," said Mamma. "It's a pet name, a loving name."

But Evvie flounced off in a huff. Heels hard on the pavement, braids quivering, she went up Bishop Street alone. When she came opposite the Ross home, did she even turn her head? No, not Evvie! She walked steadily on, two blocks, three blocks, past the borders of the campus, and along the streets to the Square. She marched to the millinery shop, mounted two steps, punched the bell, opened the door, and walked in. The milliner came from an inner room. Today she didn't seem quite so stylish, but much busier. Too busy for nonsense. Evvie felt small and chilled. But her words tumbled out in a rush.

"I have brought back the Alice blue tam," she said. "It still has the price tag on it. I haven't worn it. I would like the money back, please."

"And what is the matter with the tam, pray tell?" inquired Miss

Rupert coldly. She drew the tam from its paper bag, examining it.

"Nothing's the matter," answered Evvie, scared but determined. "It's nice. I like it. But I don't really need it . . . Yesterday," Evvie burst out, "my mother didn't buy a hat for herself. If she doesn't have one, neither must I. Don't you see? I can't. I won't. I'd hate the blue tam forever and ever. I couldn't wear it, seeing my mother in her old hat."

There was a long silence, with Evvie looking up at the milliner, and the milliner looking down at her. "Very well," said the lady, at last. She handed the refund to Evvie. She stepped to the door and opened it. She held the door as if she wanted Evvie to leave, and the sooner the better.

"Thank you, Miss Rupert," faltered Evvie, head bent meekly as she stepped to the sidewalk. Once there, she looked up. "Thank you very much," she said clearly. "I hated to ask you. I think all your hats are nice."

Suddenly the milliner smiled. It made a big difference in her looks. "Yesterday I heard them call you Evvie," she said. "Well, Evvie, come back some time and buy another hat from me. You're a girl of style and spirit."

Evvie walked home, her heart lighter not because of the milliner's compliment, but because she had done what she thought was right if she were to live with herself. At home she had to tell. That was the trouble.

At once Lizette wished ardently that she had been the one to think of making a noble sacrifice of her pretty headpiece. She even suggested it aloud. Mamma's "no" was quick, and she added, to make it stick with Lizette, "A thousand times no!"

She went on, "You took a good deal upon yourself, Evvie, in returning the tam, making yourself seem wiser than me, and not being really fair to Miss Rupert. I know your intentions were good, and in one way you did a brave, unselfish thing. But watch yourself. And girls, neither one of you is to say a word about the millinery. The boys won't notice, and Papa isn't likely to. But his pride would be hurt if he thought any sacrifice had been made. It is true he is short of cash at present. The fire on the roof was a blow. The payments on the place must be made every month. And he's very troubled as to whether his medical practice in Winfield will improve. We must all trust him and be as cheerful as possible. A better day will come. It's on its way." Mamma spoke with such certainty the girls could almost see Lady Luck hiding slyly around the corner.

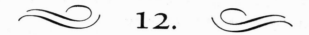

12.

Evvie Tries a Change

EVVIE was braiding her hair. Reflected in the mirror was Mamma, coming to help. Mamma tied Evvie's two braids together at the nape of the neck with a blue ribbon. The big bow stood out like wings on either side of Evvie's pale cheeks. "You're not frightened, are you?" asked Mamma gently.

"No," fibbed Evvie. In the mirror her eyes were solemn.

"The first day at a strange school is rather disturbing. Is that what bothers you?"

"A little," murmured Evvie. But it wasn't that. Evvie had always liked school. She was ready to like teachers, to adore them if they were nice. She loved meeting girls and boys her own age. They could be interesting, and fun.

But yesterday, thinking about school in Winfield, a big idea had struck Evvie. It had taken her breath. All day she thought about it. The more she thought, the more clearly she realized that today would bring a golden opportunity. She must take advantage of it before it was too late.

But she hadn't slept well last night. It was a big step to take.

It was something like returning the Alice blue tam without permission from Mamma, only much more in the spirit of I-am-Miss-Evalina-Hudson-and-I-shall-do-as-I-please. "Oh, dear," whispered Evvie to herself, "I don't mean it in that smarty way at all. But I've got to do it while I have the chance. I've got to!"

"Don't let on to Lizette that you're nervous about the first day of school. You know how shy she is, anyway." Mamma gave the ribbon bow a final tweak.

"I'll see Lizette into her room," promised Evvie. Her mouth felt dry. Dainty in a sleeveless organdy apron over her dark dress, Evvie went to the kitchen for a drink. Lizette was there for the same purpose. She wore an apron like Evvie's. Her curls shone like those of a Christmas doll.

"When you come home, I'll have something to eat that you like," promised Mamma. It was cheering. But at the front door Evvie clung to her mother. Little did Mamma dream that this September day of 1906 was marking a milestone in Evvie's life. In a way, Mamma was saying good-bye forever to Evvie Hudson.

"Be sure and get a list of all the supplies you will need," called Mamma. "I'll telephone them to Papa. This evening he will bring them home. When I was young I thought there was nothing more wonderful than the new school books. Even the fresh pencils smelled entrancing."

Mamma watched the children walking up Bishop Street. Max and Martin were so slicked up as to seem like strangers. George Akers was also unnaturally neat. All the children waved at Mamma as long as they could see her. They waved at Vasey's mother as they passed the Ross house. They said "hello" to Anna the great Dane, who trotted along, not knowing she could never go to school and learn. At the corner where the university president lived, the children turned south and walked to Emblem Street. There, in the middle of the block, stood Second Ward School.

At sight of it, Evvie drew a long, fluttering breath. But she led Lizette and the twins into the principal's office, as George advised. She presented the report cards from Fairland. The principal studied them, and before directing the children to their rooms, entered their names in his ledger. "Welcome, children," he said, "to Second Ward School. I hope you will be happy here. Try to do well in your studies."

Before climbing to the second floor, Evvie made sure that Lizette was recognized by her teacher as one who was new and shy. Upstairs, then, Evvie paused at room six for a peep. "The teacher looks nice," decided Evvie. "Stylish, too." For the lady was wearing one of the latest fashions, a gored rainy-daisy skirt. The sleeves of her shirtwaist were crisp leg-o'-mutton. Her pompadour was high and sleek. Clutching her report card, Evvie stepped inside. The faces of many children seemed but a single blur. Evvie made a wavering bee-line for the teacher's desk. "Help!" she breathed. The time had come.

Since it was the first day, school was dismissed before noon. Evvie hastened to the lower hall to join Lizette. Together the sisters skipped homeward. Evvie's skips were joyous leaps. Her braids swung. The blue bow jiggled. She had done it—without a single hitch she had done it! Evvie began singing *Waltz Me around Again, Willie*. It was a new song, very popular. "The music is dreamy, it's peaches and creamy; oh, don't let my feet touch the ground," warbled Evvie softly, and twirled on one toe.

"The other day you were saying doggone," said Lizette, having a little twirl herself.

"That was about the blue tam and Mamma having no new hat," explained Evvie. "Today it is something different." Evvie would have liked to confide in her sister. But Lizette would be likely to tattle to the family before Evvie was ready.

The girls came within sight of home. "If only the cupola was up there!" said Lizette. "You know, Evvie, I think Papa and Mamma are up to something."

"You've noticed that, have you?" Evvie was surprised, for Lizette was an off-in-another-world kind of a girl. "Well, if it's really anything important I guess we shall know when they get ready to tell us."

Evvie's words trailed off into silence. Now that she was within sight of home, she sobered. Her steps slowed. Oh my goodness, how would Mamma and Papa take it? She was glad she had done it, but she dreaded what everyone might say. It could turn into a hullabaloo.

True to her promise, Mamma had something exciting to eat. Still warm from the oven, the peach turnovers looked like neat little pastry pocket-books. A twisted braid of crust bound the edges. Inside, there was a delicious treasure of thick juicy fruit. Yummy! For a little while the turnovers not only relieved Evvie's hunger, but banished her worries.

In the afternoon she was fidgety again. She didn't even feel well. She decided to write Unc a letter. Unc was special. He should know what Evvie had done. *Dearest Unc,* began Evvie, and the rest of the brief letter was written hastily and earnestly. She ended, *I hope you won't mind. Your loving niece that used to be Evvie Hudson.*

Papa came home. The twins appeared looking as if they had been on some far distant excursion, though it was no farther than the pond. The family gathered around the table. The plates were served. Evvie's gaze roved from Papa to Mamma and back again. They were such nice people. Would they be troubled?

"Children," began Papa, "the big brown package I brought home contains your new school books. After supper we'll make some oilcloth covers to keep them clean. Remember, Martin, you are not to draw beards on the gentlemen's faces in your history book. How do all of you find school in Winfield?"

"As well as any school," answered Max.

"Same thing as in Fairland, only bigger," added Martin. "Just because we're twins, the kids called Max and me Ditto and Which-is-Which, and names like that." Martin grinned. "We didn't care. They're a pretty good bunch. Besides, we showed 'em we can take care of ourselves." Martin studied his skinned knuckles.

"H-mmmm," murmured Papa. He turned to Lizette. "What about our youngest?"

Lizette waved her fork. "My teacher's name is Miss Bliss. She smiled when I showed her how I can read. A special smile, Papa. Honest!"

"That's good news," agreed Papa. "It would be bliss if you could learn arithmetic from Miss Bliss, also. Evvie, it's your turn."

Evvie's head suddenly seemed too light. Her fork shook as she laid it carefully on her plate. "Papa!" she exclaimed, faintly. She fixed her father's attention with a solemn gaze. "Mamma!" she turned to her mother with a look pained, yet stubborn. "Please don't mind too much," she begged. "At school today I—I—today I changed my name."

"Great Scott! What to?" cried Martin.

"Toenails and teeth!" Max stared. He would no more have changed his name than shed his skin. "What to? What for?" he demanded. "You can't change your name. A person can't!"

"A person can if it's terribly important," Evvie retorted. "When I gave the teacher my report card, I said, 'Miss Copeland, there's more to the name on this card. It should be *Helen* Evalina Hudson. I'd appreciate it if you'd call me *Helen*.' And she said she would. You see, I chose *Helen* because I've always liked it and no one can shorten it. So that's who I'm planning to be from now on—Helen."

"Helen is not the name your mother and I selected for you. Your birth certificate is filed in the county courthouse as Evalina Hudson," said Papa. *"Evalina* is a beautiful name."

"But no one ever calls me that. It's always Evvie, Evvie, Evvie. I'm sick and tired of it. It's no name at all."

"The family isn't tired of it. You've been Evvie to us for almost twelve years," reasoned Mamma.

Although she had been rather bowled over by the news that she was registered in the county courthouse, other hot arguments were springing to Evvie's lips. "Then why isn't Lizette called *Lizzie?*"

Lizette tried it then and there. "I wouldn't mind," she offered. "I'll be Lizzie if you will keep on being Evvie. Please be Evvie."

"No!" cried Evvie. "Oh, don't you see, all of you, how I had to be someone more than *Evvie?* Coming to Winfield and a new school where no one knew me—it was my one chance."

"But if you had a choice, and leaving Evvie out of it, would you rather be Helen or Evalina?" asked Papa.

Evvie thought about it. "I'd rather be Evalina if I could surely be called that," she admitted, "because that's my honest-to-goodness name."

"Yes, that is your name," said Papa, "and I think you shouldn't go hiding it behind Helen. Will you forget it if we try to call you Evalina?"

"Shoot, why all the fuss?" sighed Max, looking bored.

"It's the way Evvie feels," Mamma explained. "It will be hard for us at first to call her Evalina. I will telephone Miss Copeland this evening. I will ask her to see that our child is known as Evalina at school."

Evvie flushed. "Miss Copeland will think I made up something that that wasn't exactly true," she objected.

"Not at all true, you mean," said Mamma. "You took a good deal upon yourself. Watch your ways." In spite of the reproof, Mamma smiled so warmly that Evvie ran around the table to snuggle against her shoulder.

"Evalina Hudson," murmured Mamma, her arm around Evvie's waist. "Shall we try it, family?"

But all the faces around the table wore doubtful expressions.

So Evvie was obliged to add a postscript to her letter to Unc, explaining she was not allowed to be anyone as completely different as Helen. "But I'm Evalina, Unc. *I am!*" scribbled Evvie, underlining heavily.

Dear Red-Headed Niece, answered Unc by the next mail. *You can't expect an old thirty-year-old man like me to change my ways. To me you will always be Evvie, my best girl. Your red-headed Unc.*

When Evvie's twelfth birthday arrived in early October, Unc was there. He made the journey from Torbridge tenderly bearing a paper carton. He had ordered its contents from a master baker. It was a birthday cake topped with such perfection in frosting as to take everyone's breath. Within a wreath of pink sugar roses there was a sugary inscription—*Happy Birthday, Evalina. 1894-1906.*

The cake—and the girl—deserved a small party. To Evvie's guests Lizette tattled, although innocently, "Out places and at school her name is Evalina. But at home she's Evvie."

Unc and members of the family, watching the cutting of the cake and Evvie's sudden blushes, said, in one firm voice, "She's Evalina!"

Although it presented this loyal united front to the public, the family just couldn't stop saying Evvie at home. Evvie tried both ice and fire. She tried not hearing, not answering. And she tried with Madge Ross, although gently.

"If I were to begin calling you Evalina," said Madge, with sweet stubbornness, "I think it would be because you weren't my best friend any more. And you are, Evvie, my best and dearest friend."

"Oh, Madge! Oh, Vasey!" cried Evvie. Although Mamma had said a similar thing, it seemed more meaningful coming from the blind child. After that, Evvie didn't fuss so much. For a few years, all right—Evvie! But when she was grown-up, and beautiful, she would be known by her true name. Wasn't she recorded in the county courthouse as *Evalina Hudson?*

13.

"To Catch Wild Ducks"

IN OCTOBER the maples in the south yard made it a place of glory. As the leaves fell, yellow, red and russet, the girls raked them into patterns which they said were the walls of rooms. And there on Saturdays and on week-days after school, they played house. Again Madge Ross was a contented vase, holding fall flowers and colored leaves. What did her sensitive fingers "see," wondered Evvie. She filled Vasey's lap with spicy pine and hemlock cones, with glossy nuts from the one buckeye tree, with walnuts still in their fragrant rusty hulls. Vasey fingered them and smelled them, and behind her sightless eyes, felt the delight of *knowing*.

Vasey had a private teacher who came daily to her house. But Mrs. Ross said to Evvie, "You also are a teacher to Madge. Through her play and conversation with you and your sister and brothers, she is learning things she has never known before." When Evvie happily reported this at home, Mamma said, "You, too, learn from Madge because you care for her so much. Love is a good teacher."

The days of October, windless and golden, passed into drabness. Martin and Max and George discovered that wild fowl were floating down from their southward migration to rest and feed at the pond. Max then remembered something he had once seen in Mamma's old cook-book. It was in a fascinating column entitled *Miscellaneous*. It contained useful hints, such as how to keep rope from stiffening, how to prevent pumps from freezing, how to make hens lay in winter, how to cure stammering. There were many such gems of know-how. The hint that Max remembered was immediately shared with Martin and George. They decided to try it, secretly.

To Catch Wild Ducks or Geese Alive: Soak wheat in strong alcohol and scatter where they are in the habit of feeding, and take while they are drunk. That is what the cook-book advised. The boys howled with laughter.

For the sake of furnishing alcohol, both Max and Martin were willing to sacrifice the spiders they had preserved in bottles. Hoping it would be strong enough, they soaked several handfuls of wheat and scattered it around the shores of the pond. In the October dusk they hid behind a tree and waited.

The wild ducks came down with a flutter of folding wings and a clacking of scoop-shaped bills. Some settled on the water at once. Others alighted on land, waddling awkwardly. It took these but a moment to discover the feast of scattered wheat. They began to gobble.

The boys waited, fairly holding their breath. "Lookit! Did you ever?" For the greediest firstcomers of the ducks were already beginning to stagger, even to fall over. However often they tried to right themselves, they were helpless against this strange giddiness. In a frenzy of eagerness, the boys dashed from behind the tree. Some birds were able to fly. But it was easy to snatch up the befuddled ones, the poor drunken ones.

Presently the boys were hurrying up the pasture lane. They carried two ducks apiece—six ducks in all! It was the most exciting thing they had pulled off for ages! In the henyard Max and Martin slipped their birds under a large coop they had readied. They were so pleased they scarcely noticed when George ran for home with his own booty.

The twins were late for supper. They expected a scolding, and received it. In silence they plowed steadily through the meal. Then Martin leaned back, eyes dancing. "Guess what! We've been catching ducks!" he announced.

"We've got four under the big coop!" Max explained. "Mom, we'll give 'em to you for the Thanksgiving dinner. Christmas dinner, too."

Only half-believing, the family trooped out to see the birds which huddled, sleepy and dull, behind the slats.

"However in the world did you catch four wild ducks?" That was the question the boys kept hearing, but which they would not answer. It was a secret too good to tell. "Catchin' 'em was easier than you think," said the twins, going off into fits of laughter.

November was its usual dark and rainy self. The coop which penned the ducks was moved into the henhouse. The twins gorged them with grain. They grew fat.

Unc came from Torbridge for the Thanksgiving feast, pleased at the prospect of roast wild duck. And when dinner-time came the

brace of birds, golden brown, sent forth hunger-tickling odors. Papa said grace. He took up the carving tools. The tender meat fell away from the knife.

"Now do you want to hear how we really caught the ducks?" teased Max.

So by turns the giggling twins told how they had made the ducks so drunk with wheat soaked in alcohol it was easy to pick them up. "We learned how to do it from Mamma's cook-book—the old-fashioned one," explained Martin.

Unc tipped back his head and roared. "Never heard of such a way for a couple of kids to get a Thanksgiving dinner," he said.

Papa grinned and looked at his boys as he often did, with surprise.

Mamma looked surprised also—in fact, shocked. When she thought no one was looking, she pushed aside the meat on her plate.

"The duck is excellent," Papa complimented her. Unc and the boys heartily agreed. Knives and forks were busy. Lizette, who was finicky about food, forked a small piece. "I've never tasted wild duck before," she said. "I wonder if I shall like it. Mamma doesn't. I don't think Evvie does, either."

"Great Scott, I don't see how anyone can help liking this wild duck!" declared Max. "Pop, I'll have some more, please."

"Me, too," said Martin, his mouth full.

"I might like the duck meat if I could bear to eat it." Evvie was never afraid to speak her mind. "But since you boys told us how you caught the ducks—that's what makes the difference. I think it was terrible making the poor wild creatures so drunk they hadn't a chance to fly away."

"I confess I feel that way, too," agreed Mamma. "The thought of drunken ducks takes away my appetite."

"Good heavens, girls!" cried Unc. "Wild fowl were made to eat. Men go out to shoot them every day."

"I know," argued Evvie. "Getting them that way seems more sporting. This other way—the twins' way—well, it made fools of the ducks, as it makes fools of people."

"You're mincing matters. You're being finicky." For once Unc was impatient with Evvie.

"If it had been wrong, it wouldn't have been in Mamma's cookbook!" cried Max.

Papa spoke up. "I suggest that those who have no scruples against eating the duck, and I am one, go ahead and enjoy it. Those who have different opinions—and they have the right—are not obliged to eat."

Lizette looked at the downcast faces of the twins, who suddenly realized the Thanksgiving feast was a failure. "I'll try," she offered, and began picking at the meat.

"The twins meant well," said Mamma. "It was very good of them to want to furnish part of our dinner today."

"Max and I have got another surprise for you," said Martin rather dolefully. "Only," he added, with a little spite, "maybe we oughtn't to tell you. Maybe somebody would think of some daffy reason for not liking it."

"If it's good news we shall like it," Mamma assured him.

"Max and I have a chance to work a paper route."

"We're going to put all the money we make into the cupola fund," declared Max. "Papa, may we have the route?"

"Yes," answered Papa. "It will be good for you to learn to keep accounts and to handle money you earn yourselves."

"And to be polite to your customers," added Mamma.

"Won't we just rattle them!" giggled Martin. "They won't know which of us is which."

"Now I have something to tell you," said Papa. "My medical practice is picking up a good deal. But it will be still better, because next

week I'm moving into a cottage I've rented for my office. It's on
Bishop Street near the university."

"Hooray!" cried the children. "Now you will be a busy doctor
again, as you were in Fairland."

"Some day, I hope." Papa nodded, smiling.

"By the way, John," began Unc, "how are you getting on with
the—"

But Unc received a quick glance of warning from both Papa and
Mamma. It stopped him. He never did finish the question within
hearing of the children. It made them wonder a little, and not for
the first time, what was going on. "I know it's something to do with
getting a new cupola," confided Max to his twin.

14.

Lizette and the Snow Queen

THE FIRST big snow began falling one December afternoon. By the time school was dismissed, it lay thick. To take deep steps in it was exciting. Snowballs flew. Shouts and laughter rang out. Evvie and Lizette, making their way homeward, felt almost as if they were caught up into the air with the swirling flakes.

"They look alive," mused Evvie.

"They are 'the white bees swarming,'" quoted Lizette, remembering the old grandmother's words in Andersen's story of *The Snow Queen*. The tale was one of Lizette's favorites.

Evvie laughed, pleased, at this snowy hour, to be reminded of the pretty phrase.

"Let's go coasting when we get home, shall we?" asked Lizette. "We have a hill of our own, now." She gave a hippity-hop. Her feet slid. Down she went. It only added to the fun. The girls went laughing into Cupola House.

"It is snowing too hard for coasting," Mamma said, "and I want you to help me prepare an early supper. Papa must have a long evening for some work he is doing."

The girls exchanged their white ruffled pinafores for plain gingham ones. They began to help with the supper. But whenever they could catch a moment, they stood at the windows watching the snow fall. It made them feel cozy. They saw Max and Martin plodding up the hill and into the house. "Goody!" cried Martin. "This snow is the real stuff! We'll have to wear our high boots while we deliver our papers."

"Get it over in a hurry," advised Mamma. "Listen, I hear the sound of bells."

Everyone ran to the windows in time to see Thad Conroy in a nifty bright red sleigh, skimming around the corner where Bishop Street turned into Auburn Road. On Thad's left sat Madge Ross, rosy and smiling. On his right sat Anna the Dane, looking almost as big as the horse. Anna's tongue hung out in a doggish smile of enjoyment.

Papa came home, saying, "This deep snow means that wheels must give place to runners." He and the boys went to haul out the sleigh where it would be handy for Papa's next trip. They did the evening chores before returning for Mamma's delicious supper. Throughout the meal the family was conscious of the wonder of the snow, silently piling up outside. Papa lit a crackling fire in the sitting-room grate. The boys ran for the long-handled popper, and for the corn they had shelled. It had grown in the Hudsons' own fields.

"D'you know what?" Lizette was eager. "This is the very night for reading aloud *The Snow Queen*. Please, Papa?"

"I have work to do," answered Papa. But he smiled his willingness. As he was about to open the worn volume Lizette had brought, the telephone rang. It was a call for him, and in a moment the bells on Molly's harness could be heard jingling from the lane.

So it was Mamma who read aloud Andersen's wonderful story, while the embers in the fireplace glowed red and the popcorn merrily

exploded. Lizette, munching dreamily, imagined herself drawn behind the great sledge of the Queen, faster, ever faster. When certain
parts of the story sent chills down her spine, it was quite as if she
were Kay, shivering under the freezing kiss of that terrible ice-maiden.
She went dreaming to bed.

Sometime in the night the snow ceased to fall. When morning
came, the window glass was covered with frost flowers more delicate
than any earth-grown blossoms. It was because the Snow Queen had
flown by in the night and looked in through the panes. Blowing her
breath on the flowers, Lizette rubbed the melted spot with her finger.
What she could see of the Hudson acres lay smooth and trackless.

Papa went off in the sleigh. Max and Martin cleared the walks.
They did their other chores in a hurry. They were going to a steep
hill west of town which George had told them about. But Mamma
said to the girls, "You can have good fun on our own hill. Last night
your father brought your sleds to the back porch and greased the
runners. They are ready. Take them out and enjoy yourselves."

But then Evvie said a most surprising thing. "I'm not going
coasting until I've ironed my other white apron for Monday."

How perfectly provoking of Evvie! With this exciting snow and
the sleds ready, to prefer fluting ruffles! Oh, there were times when
Evvie was altogether too sensible and grown-up!

"Then I'll go without you, Miss," pouted Lizette.

"Go ahead," answered Evvie. "I'll be out before long."

Pretending not to care, Lizette donned cloak and hood. Over her
feet and legs she drew the long oversize wool hose that Mamma had
knit for snowy weather. She pulled on her mittens. Outside, with
the rope of her sled in her hand, she turned to wave at Mamma.
Evvie wasn't even looking. Already she was busy with her silly
ruffles. I never will call her Evalina! thought Lizette angrily. Never!

Lizette not only went sliding, but three times she lay down on a glistening bank and made angel prints. She started to roll up snow to build a funny white man. But everything she did was half-hearted. She needed someone to shout and laugh with her in the cold, pure stillness. She felt lonely and disappointed.

Gazing up Bishop Street, she saw it as a narrow tunnel lying between banks piled up when sidewalks were cleared early this morning. It would be fun to go through that tunnel, thought Lizette. Maybe I could go as far as Vasey's house. I could take Vasey for a ride on my sled.

Lizette coasted down the hill once more. At the bottom, she got to her feet and pulled her sled across Auburn Road, then through the cleared ways of Bishop Street. At the next corner a horse and sleigh stood before the home of the college president. Three boys played in the street nearby. Lizette had seen them at school, but did not know their names. Now, anxious to reach Vasey's house without being spied by the boys, Lizette hardly noticed a man hurrying out from the president's house, hopping into the sleigh, calling back some message, and starting up.

One of the boys darted up to Lizette. "Want some fun?" he whispered. Laughing, he gave her a push. She tumbled backward on her sled. The boy righted her. He snatched the sled rope, looped it quickly around the cross-piece at the back of the sleigh, and made a slip knot. "Hold tight, now," he said. To her immense astonishment, Lizette and her sled were scooting off! She had a blurred glimpse of the laughing faces of the boys.

The driver of the sleigh had been intent on his own business. He had taken small notice of the playing boys. He didn't know that a little girl had arrived upon the scene, nor that she was now following him, willy-nilly, on her sled.

Everything had happened so quickly that Lizette felt dazed. Almost at once, however, she began to be uneasy. If she had only stayed

on the Hudson hill! By this time Evvie was perhaps ready to play. And what would Mamma think if she could see Lizette skimming away—no telling where—behind a stranger? Still, if Lizette weren't taken too far, it might be fun. She would have something to relate to Evvie. Feeling alarmed one moment and adventurous the next, Lizette flew past Vasey's house. Opposite Papa's new office, she had a moment of real panic. "Stop!" she demanded. Her voice was but a thin quaver amid the merry clamor of the bells. At College Avenue the sleigh made a swift turn. Lizette almost fell off her sled. At Washington Street came another turn. The sleigh sped into the Square. Surely, at this center of Saturday activity, the driver would stop.

But he circled the courthouse rapidly. He turned out of the
Square into the northern part of town. The houses grew fewer. Horse
and sleigh headed for the country. Lizette opened her mouth again.
Not a squeak came out of it. She was too dreadfully timid, too fearful. And she felt ashamed of having been tricked into such crazy
adventure by that boy in town. Oh, sensible Evvie would have
managed all of this so differently!

Lizette stared up at the black fur cap and broad dark shoulders
which was all she could see of the driver. Who was he? And suddenly
she felt quite frozen with fright. Could he be the Snow Queen who
had disguised herself as a man? Could the Snow Queen be taking
Lizette Hudson north to the vast and empty halls of her ice palace?

Oh, how silly! The Snow Queen lived only in a fairy tale. Still—

Then, to save herself, Lizette must roll off her sled. But it was
precious. She would lose it. She herself might lie lost and frozen in
a snow drift. For all about her stretched the wide-spread loneliness
of the snow-covered land. While the sleigh bells shook out their merry
music, Lizette's tears rolled down her cheeks.

Suddenly the man in the sleigh began to sing. His voice boomed
out over the snowy fields.

> *Yankee Doodle keep it up*
> *Yankee Doodle dandy*
> *Mind the music and the step,*
> *And with the girls be handy.*

Surely the Snow Queen, cruel, cold and certainly *not* an American,
would never know a song like *Yankee Doodle*. Yet couldn't she be
cleverly letting on just to fool everybody? "I don't care who you
are!" screamed Lizette, suddenly. "I'm here!"

The driver turned, startled. He saw the small, muffled figure on
the sled, the tearful face. He pulled on the reins, jumped out of the

sleigh and came around to stare down at Lizette. "Pop my eyes!" he cried. "Where did *you* come from?"

"A boy in Winfield tied me on. I want to go home. My mother—" When the man leaned to help her off her sled, Lizette struggled. "You might be the Snow Queen!" she croaked.

"Pop my ears, Sis, I don't know what you're talking about. I'm no queen. My name is Al Dobson, and I live in a town about twenty miles north of here. I'm anxious to get there. Let's see, now. There's a farmhouse up the road a piece. You just sit beside me in the sleigh till we reach it. Then I'll hop out and see about some way of getting you back to Winfield. At least we can phone your folks."

Al had a kind face, and his sensible talk furnished Lizette a sliver of comfort. Seated beside him, with the buffalo robe tucked around her, Lizette let out a long breath. She flexed her stiff wrists.

Halting at the farmhouse, Al Dobson hurried Lizette to the door and knocked. He explained matters to the farmer who answered, and to the wife and their son Joel. He had their promise to look after Lizette until she could somehow be fetched home.

"I want to go right now," she insisted, when the door had closed on Al. Home was her one thought. She begrudged the time spent in telling her name. She had to tell what the Winfield boy had done, and how she had flown through town and country. "Gee, the ride must've been fun!" remarked Joel, longingly.

Fun! Lizette shook her head. "How soon shall we start?" she inquired.

"First you must get warmed up," declared the housewife. She removed Lizette's wraps, and seated her close to a big baseburner stove. While Lizette toasted, and was refreshed with hot milk and bread-and-butter, the farmer folk discussed her. They looked up Dr. John Hudson's name in the telephone book. But then the housewife argued, "Maybe there would be none of her folks who could come after the child very soon. So there's no need of raising a scare for them."

"By this time my mother is worried about me," ventured Lizette. "She'd like to know where I am."

"Don't fret, child. It's only three miles to town. We'll soon get you there. Henry," said the wife to her husband, "you must hitch up the buggy and take Lizette and her sled back to Winfield. While you're there, will you buy some staples at the grocery? I have a list."

"Pa, could I go, too?" begged Joel.

Within the half-hour Joel and Lizette were squeezed into the narrow buggy with the farmer. The sled was tied on behind. The horse plodded through the snow with effort. The wheels turned slowly. How different it was from Lizette's swift journey behind runners! But at least she was homeward bound. Home!

15.

The Secret

BY THE time the horse and buggy had reached the town Square, it was easy to see that Joel had something on his mind.

"Pa," he began, "why don't you stop and begin buying the groceries Ma wants? I'll haul the little girl the rest of the way on her sled. I know the way. It's not too far, and I can do it in a hurry. Look, Pa, it's beginning to snow again. We can save time, 'cause when I come back you'll have your buyin' done, and we can get home." Then Joel added the real argument. "It will be fun," he said. "A guy doesn't get to Winfield every day. I'd like to see the town kids hitching rides behind sleighs."

To the farmer it sounded reasonable. Joel was twelve years old, and a boy who could be trusted. Let him have fun, thought the farmer.

The sled was untied. Lizette, helpless but hopeful, took her seat. Joel started pulling her around the Square, gazing with a country boy's interest at the Saturday shoppers, and the movement around the courthouse. Snow was falling in a fine mist. But now it thickened into a blinding flurry borne on a sudden gale. Lizette ducked her head against it. And in that helpless moment she sensed that Joel had quickly left the sidewalk. He was tying the sled's rope to a sleigh just leaving the post-office. Flinging himself to his knees behind Lizette, he said in her ear, "Scoot forward, will you, and give me room? Hold on, now!" His voice was full of glee. As the sleigh moved forward, his grip on Lizette's shoulders was painful.

The driver's horse was fast. When Lizette's wits cleared, she cried out, "Joel, you don't know where the man is going! I want to go home. You promised."

"We'll cast off if he takes the wrong direction," Joel assured her. "Don't worry. We'll have a jolly ride for a little while, anyway." *Jolly!* Lizette wanted to yell back something really mean. Now the sleigh was skimming past the college campus, and above the gay jingle of sleigh bells, the clock boomed out the time . . . *ONE,* and the echo . . . *TWO,* and the echo . . . How mournful it sounded to Lizette! "Joel!" she wailed.

The man in the sleigh heard. He turned around to peer through the blizzard. Two children out for a lark, the little girl so hunched over that he could not see her face. The boy was a stranger. And to the children the driver appeared like other men this snowy day—a fur cap, the ends of a bright muffler flying, a pair of warmly clad shoulders sprinkled with flakes.

"We're goin' the right way, you betcha," chuckled Joel. Lizette felt assured. But how she ached! How tired and dazed she felt! It was hard to keep from crying again. Sleigh and sled seemed to skim through the snow-thick air.

Suddenly, with a final shake of bells, the sleigh stopped. Lizette almost fell forward on her nose. Joel tumbled sideways into a drift. The driver jumped out. That face! Lizette's mouth fell open, and for a moment she couldn't speak. "Papa!" she breathed. Through the snow beyond him a big white barn loomed up. There was a big white house on a snowy terrace. Home! Right through town, right down Bishop

Street, *spang* up the Hudson lane, Papa, all unknowing, had brought Lizette home!

"Bless my soul!" he cried, staring down at her. "Where have you been?" He helped her to her feet and tried to hurry her toward the house. But she was too stiff to hurry. Then she remembered Joel. She looked back. There he was, still half-buried in the drift, red-cheeked with cold, round-eyed with astonishment.

"Who's he?" demanded Papa.

"He's Joel," answered Lizette, and she added, "he's a friend." For suddenly it did seem that Joel was a friend of sorts. Hadn't he hitched on, though, purely by chance, to the right sleigh?

Invited into the house, Joel stood awkward and shy. But he was interested in seeing Lizette's relatives, and the relief and happiness on their faces. He helped to make clear what had happened to Lizette as far as he knew it. He grinned all the time, for to him her adventures seemed highly amusing.

Lizette was unwrapped and her hands rubbed. She was told by both parents how foolish and wrong she had been to go off to Bishop Street this morning without permission. "All the rest of her adventures were accidental," decided Mamma, "although she should have been courageous enough to make herself heard before being carried so far." Papa ordered a warm drink for her, and a dose of medicine. "She must spend the rest of the afternoon in bed. She will sleep. And she will think. Sometimes thinking does much good, even when it comes too late."

At that Joel sobered up and gazed at Lizette with pity. Bed in mid-afternoon seemed like real punishment. He said, "I must go and find my pa in the Square." Before leaving he was given thanks and a box of molasses cookies. Evvie gave him a big smile for bringing back her little sister. Max and Martin took him upstairs and presented him with two thrilling bones from their collection. Papa said he would take

Joel to the Square. "I've made three trips back and forth today looking for Lizette," he said. "One more won't matter."

After a warm bath, a cup of hot chocolate, and a dosage, Lizette
was undressed and put to bed in Mamma's downstairs sleeping-room.
That was a treat in itself. Under the covers her feet nudged the hot
water bottle, but gently, because on the counterpane, at the foot of the
bed, lay Evvie's white apron, its ruffles fluted to perfection. Lizette
lay in warm silence, while the fire on the hearth threw dancing lights
on ceiling and walls.

Presently, through a fog of sleepiness, she saw Evvie come in and
whisk away the apron. "Wait," murmured Lizette. "I am glad to
see you again, Evalina." She went on, her voice trailing away. "I
can't remember that man's name. But, Evalina, he was not the Snow
Queen." Evvie smiled at Lizette in the motherly way she often smiled
at Vasey. Lizette's eyes closed. Home! she thought. Home!

She slept through the supper hour. When she woke, Evalina
brought her a tray of food. She felt special, eating daintily in bed, and
said so. "I guess you are pretty special today," admitted Evvie. Max
and Martin peeped in merrily to greet her. Then Papa came. He took
Lizette's temperature and pronounced her fit. He closed the door and
sat down by the bed. Lizette thought she was in for some serious talk
about her sins.

"You know," Papa began, "that 'most everyone thinks you are a girl
who tells everything she knows—a girl who can't keep a secret.
I believe you can. That's partly why I'm going to tell you
one—a big one. You will be the only person who knows it besides Mamma and Unc and some people in New York. It's not
that I'm keeping it from the other children in favor of you.
Sooner or later we shall tell them. But it was a remark of yours
which gave your mother the idea. She passed it on to me." So then,

while the fire whispered on the hearth, Papa whispered the secret to Lizette.

She sat straight up in bed and flung her arms around Papa's neck. "Oh, I can't wait to see it finished! I can't wait! Papa, I would love to tell this wonderful secret to everybody. But you needn't worry. This is a secret I wouldn't tell for anything in the world, cross-my-heart-and-hope-to die!"

16.

Holidays and Happenings

THE children placed pumpkin and sunflower seeds on window-ledges. The birds wintering around the house came to feed. The flutter of their wings was often reflected in the window-panes.

Three days before Christmas came another snow. It did not last long, but was borne on a strong sleety gale. Papa had asked Mr. Van Winkle to help the twins drag a tree into the sitting-room. While they were at it, with George Akers helping, and Mamma and the girls on the sidelines, an odd thing happened.

Slowly through the open door came the tree. Furiously blew the sleet. And riding right into the house with it soared a chickadee. It was as if the bird could not help itself, or else it was following the tree. Once inside, with the door closed to keep out wind and weather, the tiny bird fluttered in panic against ceiling and walls. Sometimes it alighted on door lintels, picture frames, or the corner whatnot. Evvie ran to telephone Vasey. "You can't guess," said Evvie. "We have a Christmas tree and a Christmas bird."

When the tree stood upright on its base, the chickadee flew in among the branches. There it hopped about and hid itself, and seemed rather at home. On the sheet beneath the tree the children placed water and crumbs. They sat at the edges of the room, scarcely moving. "It isn't every day a bird flies into our house and lives with us, is it?" And they resolved, rather than frighten the chickadee, to leave the tree untrimmed. It was forest-beautiful in itself, thick and plumy, dark green and fragrant.

Evvie decided to make popcorn balls. "Thunderation!" cried Max. "We'll sell 'em to the folks on our paper routes and add to the cupola fund." From that time until the balls were finished, there seemed to be double the number of Hudson children in the kitchen, as all tried to take a hand or give advice. "Don't make any mistakes, Evvie," said Martin, shelling corn with might and main. "Remember that mush!"

"The mush was your making, too," retorted Evvie.

The popped corn was piled high in a pan, fluffy-white as a snow drift. Evvie boiled the molasses syrup to the correct stage. She poured it over the corn and formed the balls. "I will save one ball for Vasey," she announced.

"One for Mrs. Van Winkle, please," begged Lizette.

"One for George and one for Unc," advised Max.

"Two for Unc. He will need two." Evvie's eyes danced as if she knew a secret.

"I s'pose you mean that Unc's a big man and can easily hold two popcorn balls," guessed Max.

The balls sold well among the newspaper customers. The twins did further business. They exchanged the ducks for a Christmas turkey at a downtown butcher shop. "Who says we're not pretty slick?" crowed Martin.

"Nobody says it," snickered Max, "so I guess we'd better keep still about it ourselves."

On the day before Christmas, Vasey's father telephoned to ask if he might bring her to "see" the chickadee. It worried the children to think that the blind child might not even hear the bird stir among the tree branches or fly about the room. For her sake, Max turned everyone out and managed to close down on the bird with his butterfly net. By the time Vasey arrived, it was a prisoner in a wicker basket.

Max reached in, lifted out the fluttering four-inch creature, and transferred it to Vasey's cupped hands. To see her delight made everyone want to laugh for joy and to cry for tenderness. Within her gentle grasp, the bird huddled soft and quiet, as if it knew she loved it. Presently, of her own free will, she opened her fingers. "Fly," she whispered. For a moment the bird waited, a tiny bundle of feathers. Then Vasey felt the light prick of claws, the delicate leap. "I shall never forget," she murmured, and she cupped one empty palm over the other, as if, like holding the chickadee, she could hold the memory in her hand.

That evening, as the Hudsons were filing out of the house to attend church, the chickadee flew over their heads into the winter dark. The children were half-sorry, half-glad. It was wonderful to stay up later than usual that night trimming the tree, making Christmas magic.

The next morning dawned sunny. The children found their tree hung with simple gifts. Papa seemed as pleased as Santa himself to present Mamma with a new hat. Remembering her, Miss Rupert had trimmed it with luscious velvet flowers in blue, violet and lavender. "And Papa!" squealed Evvie, scrabbling around amid tissue-paper. "Here's the Alice blue tam I took back to the milliner—the very same!"

The children missed Unc. Usually he arrived on Christmas Eve. This time, for some reason, he had postponed his coming. At mid-morning of Christmas Day he was seen coming up the front walk. But someone was with him. Who was she?

She was a tall, stylish young lady. Her hair was a dark cloud around her face. She had fine dark smiling eyes. Papa and Mamma were as surprised as anyone at her coming. But Evvie said, "I knew. That's why I said we must save two popcorn balls for Unc. He wrote to me—just me—that he was bringing a friend today." And Evvie added, boasting in spite of herself, "I can keep a secret."

"So can I," declared Lizette.

Evvie giggled. The twins snorted.

"I can!" cried Lizette. "I've been keeping a *terrific* secret for a long time!" The boys dared her to tell it. For a moment she was in mortal danger of it. By clenching her teeth and tightening her jaw, the secret stayed inside.

"Hey, Evvie!" Max whispered. "D'you think Unc's really got a sure-enough girl?"

"I don't know," Evvie admitted. Up to now Unc had shown devotion only to the Hudsons.

Unc called the young lady by her first name—Cleo. The children were shy of her style and beauty, and because her coming made Unc seem strange to them. But she soon had Evvie swooning with pure pleasure. "Evalina," said Cleo in her kind, pretty voice. Never once did she say Evvie.

"Oh, I hope Unc marries Cleo!" whispered the young redhead.

"Yes," agreed Lizette. "Cleo is beautiful. I want her for my aunt!"

"Toenails and teeth!" growled Max, and Martin echoed him. Evvie and Lizette were certainly rushing matters. Why, they'd just barely met Cleo. Acquiring a new aunt takes time and care. Even the idea of it takes some getting used to. Privately the twins cornered Unc. Jerking their thumbs in the direction of the kitchen, where Cleo was helping Mamma with the dinner, they demanded of him, "Is she your girl? You going to marry her?"

Unc grinned, then sighed. "You might ask *her*," he advised, though unwisely. "Then maybe I'd know."

Late in the day, the boys managed a moment with Cleo. By this time they felt better acquainted with her. Even so, they squirmed and blushed and finally stuttered it out. "Are you Unc's sure-enough girl?"

Cleo's red lips curved into a smile. But then she sighed, and her gaze was so dark and deep as to fairly stagger the twins. "You had better ask *him*," answered Cleo. "Then maybe I'd know."

So the boys were no wiser than before. "Grown-ups are funny people," they told one another, after Unc and Cleo had left for Torbridge.

So the first Christmas spent by the Hudsons in Winfield was both more surprising and bountiful than had been expected.

New Year's Day was quiet. Too quiet, thought the children, for Papa spent most of it in the library with the doors closed. "What's Papa doing?" inquired Evvie.

"He's working," answered Mamma.

"Sh-hhh! He's working on—" Lizette bit her lips. To keep herself from saying more, she ran to the Van Winkle cottage.

"Just think, it's 1907 now!" Lizette reminded her neighbor.

"Yes, indeedy, that's what I've written in my day book."

Lizette leaned closer to see for herself, and as usual, read on. Then didn't she stare!

I was talking to my friend Mis Field on the fone, Mrs. Van had written. *Some time back I told her about Lizette Hudson how she can read like a grown up. Mis Field sed her eyes was bad and not getting better and she misses reading more than ennything. She wundered if Lizette would come to read to her and she would pay Lizette for it.*

Lizette got just that far in the day book when her questions began tumbling out. Open-mouthed, she listened to the answers, and gasping good-bye, flew home on feet that barely touched earth. She burst into the house.

"I've got a job, Mamma, an honest-to-goodness job. I'm to get honest-to-goodness pay for it. I want to do it. Mamma, the twins sell vegetables and pop corn balls and newspapers and they catch ducks. Evvie helps at home so we don't need a hired girl and she gives up new hats and things. I haven't done anything much. Please, Mamma!"

Sister and brothers stared at Lizette as if they had never seen her before. Mamma went into the library and talked to Papa. She telephoned Mrs. Van Winkle. She telephoned Mrs. Field, and came back to report.

"I've learned that Mrs. Field lives alone, and is really hungry for books and papers. So it would be a kindness, Lizette, if you could sometimes read to her. With Papa's consent, I agreed to let you do it, perhaps once a week, but not for pay. However, Mrs. Field refused that arrangement. 'I won't have the child reading to me out of kindness only,' she said firmly. 'It might turn out to be somewhat of a chore for her. If she's willing, I can pay her fifty cents an hour.' So that's the way it was left. Lizette, Mrs. Field lives in the next block, in that tall house with the cedars."

"We deliver papers there," said Martin. "The lady's got an English bulldog with the meanest face you ever laid eyes on."

Lizette's heart skipped a beat. "I shan't be afraid of the bulldog," she declared in a small voice.

"Great Scott!" cried Martin. "Lizette Hudson, who believes in fairies! Our littlest, with a job at fifty cents an hour! Hey, Lizette, will you put your money into the cupola fund?"

"Of course," answered Lizette. "And listen, Marty! I don't think I really believe in fairies now. It's just that I believe *any* story while I'm reading it—you know, like *Little Women* or *Five Little Peppers* or *The Snow Queen*."

The very next Saturday Max himself respectfully escorted Lizette to Mrs. Field's door, and waited until it seemed fairly certain the English bulldog would not take a nip out of her.

The dog's name was *Sweetie*. While he was as ugly as sin, he was too old and fat and lazy to be fierce. Lizette soon discovered that he had a very bad breath, and she always sat as far from him as possible. The house was dark and stuffy. Mrs. Field had a long solemn face. She had little to say. She never seemed to get hungry, so there were no cookies. Not ever! Accustomed to family gaiety, Lizette felt home-sick even before she knocked on the Field door. Between times, she dreaded going. If it hadn't been for the reading, which she enjoyed and Mrs. Field loved—if it hadn't been for those half-dollars—Lizette couldn't have kept it up. But she went bravely once a week.

"Our Lizette is growing up," said Papa, proudly. "She's thinking of others at last; someone beside herself."

17.

Good News

ONE February morning Mamma told the children that Mr. Van Winkle had given Papa the name of a good building contractor. "After supper this evening," said Mamma, "this man—Emmett Giles —is coming to talk with us about building the new cupola."

It was the best news ever! Max jumped to his feet and began prancing around the breakfast table. The other children followed him in laughing parade.

When they had settled down again, Evvie said it must have been the secret Lizette had been keeping. "Not exactly," answered Lizette, hugging herself. "But the new cupola does have something to do with the secret."

"A good deal," said Papa. "The secret goes far in paying for the cupola."

Evvie and the twins looked so puzzled that Papa laughed and said he wouldn't keep them in the dark much longer. "After Emmett Giles leaves this evening I'll tell you what's been cooking," he promised.

"It must be something good," guessed Evvie, "because you and

Mamma and Lizette look so happy."

"Who isn't tickled pink that we're going to have a new cupola at last?" cried Max.

The children were all eyes and ears during that evening hour of conversation between their parents and Emmett Giles. "I can build the new cupola like the former one," said Emmett, "for I see by the engraving in this old county atlas just how it looked. I might even make *my* creation a little fancier. This is a handsome house. Nothing is too good for it."

So the contractor promised to come back soon to measure and examine and figure. "I can't start the job before mid-March, though. By that time the weather will be more settled, and I and my helpers can work steadily."

When Emmett had gone, Papa lit a fire in the library. "This seems a suitable place to tell you children what we've been holding back until we were sure it would succeed," he said. "Twins, bring some apples from the cellar, and we'll settle down for a cozy time."

As Papa began, firelight tinted more brightly the hues of the books lining the walls. "You know, children, how you've always loved the story of Tig. Several months ago Lizette said she intended making a book out of it when she grows up. Well, that remark gave Mamma the idea that I might do it while I had a good deal of spare time."

"I felt sure he could," interrupted Mamma. "I remembered the short stories he wrote while he was studying medicine."

"Papa! You've written Tig's story?" cried Evvie, eyes sparkling.

"Hush! Let Papa go on," commanded Martin.

"Yes, I've written it," answered Papa, smiling. "A New York publisher has seen my outline. He has read and liked my first seven chapters. On New Year's Day, in this room, I finished the manuscript. It has been typed by one of the college students, and sent to the publisher. I've had my advance fee—a sum about the size of

the cupola-to-be." Papa laughed. "So *The Story of Tig* will be out in book form early in May. I hope you children will like it. You will find it much longer. There's more to it."

Of course there were simply not enough of the right kind of words to say how wonderful Papa's news seemed. *The Story of Tig* in a book! Sharing with hundreds of readers a favorite Hudson story!

"I had more than one reason for telling Lizette about it first," Papa explained. "As I said a moment ago, it was she who gave us the idea. I needed to ask if she minded if I took it over."

Lizette flushed, not only because of Papa's courtesy, but because she had seen the twins nudge one another. She lifted her head and spoke with dignity. "I know of course that Papa is the one to write the book. It would have been a long time before I'm old enough."

"Bet you could have someday, though," declared Martin, switching over to faith and loyalty. And everyone looked at Lizette as if it were quite likely she would sometime whip up one successful book after another.

Papa leaned back, smiling. "Another thing," he said, "it has often been claimed that Lizette can't keep a secret. I wanted to test her with a big one. She has kept it!"

Mamma reached over and hugged Lizette. The other children sent her such admiring glances as to erase forever all memories of Lizette's old habits of tattling.

"Papa, shall you be a book-writer now, instead of a doctor?" inquired Evvie.

"No," answered Papa. "I'd rather be a doctor any day. I've said it before and I say it again."

"Papa's practice has picked up very well since he moved his office," said Mamma. "The college students are coming to him. He's being talked about as a good doctor for children."

What an evening it was! "I feel stuffed with all the good news packed inside of me," declared Martin, when he and Max were in bed.

"I bet I won't sleep a wink," answered Max.

Within five minutes he was snoozing like a woodchuck in its hole.

How welcome was the sound of hammer and saw after the carpenters arrived to build the new cupola! To the children the work seemed to drag. But at last it was finished. The contractor had indeed gone a little fancy, as he had threatened. Around the base of the cupola he had built a charming little balcony with a prettily carved railing. He had made the window-frames more ornate. New flooring was laid in the attic. A new ladder, with a hand rail and wider steps, led to the cupola. Plastering and papering was done on the second floor. The reeky smell of the fire passed away when a crew of painters went to work. Except for the window shutters and trim, the whole house was given a coat of white paint. Amid the leafing foliage of April, it fairly sparkled. "Now we can honestly call it Cupola House again," rejoiced the children.

"The cupola is yours," said Papa. "With your earnings, you helped to build it."

"We should have a big party in celebration," declared Evvie.

"In honor of Papa's book, too," agreed Lizette.

"With fireworks!" The twins meant it whole-heartedly.

"We *are* going to have a party," cried Mamma. "We're going to have a wedding!"

"Unc and Cleo?"

"Yes, Unc and Cleo. They want to be married here in early May. It's to be a simple wedding, with only a few guests. Cleo doesn't have any close relatives. So now for the wedding I shall have extra sewing and the spring housecleaning to do. The time is short. I shall need the help of all."

"There's school," Evvie pointed out. "If we only had Addy Newton now!"

"Write to her, daughter," advised Papa. "Ask her to come."

In about a week Addy arrived. She was worth waiting for. She was plain and lanky, but her eyes were so amazingly blue they actually twinkled *blue* twinkles, very kind and merry. In a trice she was in soapsuds to her elbows. "I do love weddings!" she declared. "We'll have this house as shinin' bright as the bride herself!"

Addy said she had been born "work-brickle"; a cake of soap in one hand, and a cooking-spoon in the other. The children half-believed her. They could scarcely wait for mealtimes, to see what delicious dish Addy would serve. Every day after school they noticed how the house gleamed with new cleanliness. Mamma's face smoothed out. Everyone and everything made her laugh.

She laughed when the children begged Addy to stop scrubbing and cooking long enough to visit the cupola. "Guess I might spare a minute," Addy finally agreed. She took the flight three steps at a time. The youngsters were almost winded trying to keep up. But in the cupola she gave a gasp. Planting her hands on her hips, she turned her sea-blue gaze on the view, as if sky and earth had suddenly become new and astonishing. "Whirl me 'round if this don't beat the Dutch," she exclaimed. "This beats all."

And of course it did.

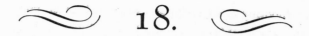

18.

Cupola House

CLEO arrived, starry-eyed. She carried a suitcase, a huge hat-box, and her wedding gown in a special container.

Unc came two days later. Not by trolley car or train, either! He came steering his own shiny black automobile, and his arrival in it marked one of the greatest moments in the history of the Hudson family. How many youngsters of 1907 had an uncle who owned an automobile!

The car was a limousine model. Unc was as pleased with it as a boy with a marvelous mobile toy. He said it was a White Steamer, so-named because it ran by steam and was manufactured by the White Sewing Machine Company. To the awe-stricken children this made Unc's auto an elegant though distant cousin of Mamma's sewing machine in the little room upstairs.

Everyone in the neighborhood came to view the Steamer. The twins and George spent all their waking hours exploring every inch of it. They dusted the leather upholstery over and over. They polished the gleaming silver-trimmed carriage lamps that adorned either side until Unc advised them to lay off, or there wouldn't be any lamps left.

Unc invited nieces and nephews, George, Madge and Thad Conroy out for a joy ride. There was a fidgety ten-minute wait while the engine worked up steam power. Then Unc moved a lever, grasped the wheel, and with a gentle *whuff-whuff* the White Steamer moved forward as smoothly and quietly as a summer breeze. How absolutely strange and unbelievable—riding up Bishop Street without a horse in front!

Unc and Evvie and Thad were in the front seat which was open at the sides. The others occupied the enclosed back, gazing out of plate-glass windows like royalty, or at least as high in the social scale as Theodore Roosevelt's children. For Unc said it was this same kind of steamer which had been chosen by the President as the official

White House car. Golly-joe, that made the young Hudsons feel like best people, and then some! This morning, all along the way, they could see Winfield residents rushing to doors and windows to watch them pass. Yelling boys and barking dogs ran alongside the car, raising a great ruckus. Unc drove slowly because of them, also because he knew that an automobile was a nightmare that unhinged the brain of any and every 1907 horse. Although he steamed gently around the courthouse square, horses danced and plunged and reared at their hitching racks. Men stepped out of shops and offices to quiet the steeds and to view the White Steamer's exciting interruption to the day's business.

Unc drove into the country. "Now we can really let 'er out," he gloated. "I'll show you what a sizzler she is!" He speeded up to a thrilling forty-five, although "she" had it in her to go even faster. Unc added that steam cars were famous for skimming up hills. "Like rabbits," he boasted. The passengers clamored for a hill to rise up before them, but about that time they neared a house that looked familiar to Lizette.

"It's where Joel lives!" she screamed. And there he was! Though he was about half an acre away, the Hudsons could see that he was dancing with excitement. He must have yelled, for his parents appeared. All three hung over the fence, watching the approach of an outlandish machine, and the cloud of dust that followed it.

Unc declared he was thirsty. He stopped the car, and everyone climbed out. They trooped through the gate and drank at the farmer's pump. They were obliged to stay five minutes while he told Unc what he thought about automobiles, which was not good. By prying and insisting he learned the price paid for the White Steamer, and was shocked, as he had hoped to be. "You're a reckless free spender," he told Unc. "Some day you will come to terrible want."

Unc grew pretty tired of such talk. He edged himself and his passengers back to the car and seated them. "I'll show the old sage a stunt that will make his eyes pop," muttered Unc. He moved the lever ever so slightly, then, to everyone's surprise, walked down the road. About five fence posts ahead, he turned. Eyes twinkling, he called out, "Come, Fido." Crooking his finger he whistled as if to a dog. And lo and behold, the White Steamer started up! Gently, slowly, it trundled toward Unc. Farmer, wife, son, and all the passengers in the moving car were frozen with astonishment. Magic, pure magic! A machine that could see, hear and obey!

When the car reached Unc, he hopped into the driver's seat, almost beside himself with glee. He was about to push the lever to give the car more power when Joel came pounding behind. Red-cheeked and goggle-eyed, but unafraid, he stammered out a demand for a ride. Unc agreed. Joel squeezed into the already crowded back seat, although over the home fence his mother was screaming her fearful objections. After about a mile of tongue-tied pleasure for Joel, Unc turned around, rode back, and Joel restored the boy to his half-fainting mother. He didn't even notice her. His eyes were on that marvelous machine. Oh, unforgettable day!

On the way to Winfield, Unc explained the stunt. "When a steam car is stopped, the engine stops, too," he said. "It cools off. Ours cooled only partly in the short time we were in the farmer's yard. So when I moved the lever a weeny bit there was time, while I walked down the road, for the engine to warm enough to move the car. I'd seen that stunt performed in Torbridge. I had tested it myself so I could spring a surprise on you."

Thad and the boys shouted with laughter. The girls didn't really understand, and the stunt still seemed like magic, but they giggled anyway. Everyone began making such crazy talk that Unc could scarcely see the road for tears of laughter. The White Steamer zig-zagged as if it couldn't see straight, either. It was a hilarious trip home, so wonderful that the children wished Unc would invite them, as well as Cleo, on the honeymoon trip.

The first copy of Papa's new book arrived. Oh, to hold it in proud and loving hands! To see *The Story of Tig* printed on the cover, and Papa's name on the title page! To see the dedication Papa had written!

To my wife Edith
and to my children
Evalina, Maxwell, Martin
and Lizette

Of course the book must be read aloud at once. Unc did it before an audience which again included Vasey and George and Thad. The reading took all evening, a wonderful time of intense listening, of laughter and tears. While the children knew that Papa could do almost anything, it did seem almost unbelievable he could have written the story that was printed in that book. They went to bed in a dream.

The Winfield newspaper printed big headlines. CRITICS PRAISE LOCAL DOCTOR'S NOVEL. The telephone rang constantly. Papa was asked to speak before an advanced English class at the university. Suddenly a good many people wanted his medical attention. Mamma was invited to join a literary club considered sacred by a number of Winfield ladies. And the craziest, most far-fetched thing—at school the Hudson youngsters were asked for their autographs! It made them giggle and blush, but at the same time rather foolishly thrilled them. Lizette read in Mrs. Van's day book: *P.D. went fishing at Klondyke. Caught 8 Catfish. Doc' Hudson has wrote a Novil. His brother has bought an automobeel for going on his Honeymoon. I planted Sweet Peas. Filled my Fountain Pen.*

"In spite of all the fuss raised hither and yon over *The Story of*

Tig," laughed Unc, "Cleo and I are still intending to have a wedding."

"Indeed, yes!" cried Mamma, radiantly happy.

So there was a wedding. Just as the ceremony began, the college clock struck three notes, sweet and solemn in the clear May air. *Three*—thought Lizette—a magic number in all fairy tales.

The beautiful bride became Aunt Cleo the moment she said "I do" and had the ring slipped on her finger. She had no bridesmaids, but Evalina in blue, Lizette in pink, and Vasey in pale green preceded her down the long stairs and stood near her before the library windows. They carried wands of blossoming plum. Max and Martin were slicked up in their best. They kept darting glances at George, making certain he was impressed to the nth degree.

Thad Conroy was Unc's attendant. Outside on the sunny terrace, Anna the great Dane guarded house and grounds. Mrs. Van Winkle, unusually pink-sugarish, beamed plumply on everyone. P.D. the woodcutter wore his hat the entire time. The children had learned long ago it was because he had no hair and was sensitive about it. There were other friends from Winfield, Fairland, and Torbridge. Addy poised tensely at the edge of things, ready to fly off to the kitchen and boss the maids hired to serve the refreshments.

There was the party. Then Thad and Papa carried out the luggage. Unc brought the White Steamer around to the end of the south walk. He came back for his bride. Everyone trooped along to see that she was safely seated. Unc climbed in, gave all his kin a fond and final look, and moved the lever. *Whuff-whuff*. Dog Anna was suddenly beside herself, dashing away and back again, with tremendous barks. With a smooth *whoosh* the limousine glided away. Cleo, a veil tied around her big hat, turned laughingly and waved. "Thanks for the wedding. Thanks for the beautiful silver tea set. Good-bye, everyone. Good-bye, Evalina."

The guests departed. The hired maids left. Addy began banging about in the kitchen.

"Addy, *really*!" protested Mamma. "Who wants to pitch in working the minute the wedding is over? The girls and I will help you if you will only wait."

"Enjoy yourselves. I am," called Addy, merrily.

"It's such a pretty day," laughed Mamma, "and I feel romantic. Let's walk out together and look at spring popping up." So the family went for a tour of the place.

"After the wedding and Unc's automobile and Aunt Cleo saying *good-bye Evalina*, I'd feel awfully let down right now if we didn't have so much left," confessed Evvie.

"You mean Papa's book and the new cupola, don't you?" Lizette skipped joyfully.

"She means much more than that," Mamma said. "Remember what I said when we first came?"

"Let me tell!" cried Martin. "You said, 'Come what will, this is a house where we shall be happy.'"

"And we are!" declared Lizette with another skip.

"We are!" Papa's voice was deep.

"When the old cupola burned, I thought I'd never be happy again," said Max. "But now—"

The Hudsons gazed up at the roof top. The new cupola rose high. It was an ornamental dome, a pretty glass hat, a fairy tower, a lookout. It was the perfect finish, orderly and balanced, not only to a dwelling, but to family faith and unity. It was the crown to CUPOLA HOUSE.